Buried Secrets

Book 4 of Shady Woods

J Mercer

Published 2023 / Bare Ink

Printed in the United States of America

E-ISBN: 979-8-9872567-4-9

Paperback ISBN: 979-8-9872567-5-6

Hardcover ISBN: 979-8-9872567-6-3

BURIED SECRETS / written by J Mercer

Cover design by Jim Mayfield

Contents

Chapter One

She Got the Cellar

I was magnetically attracted to him.

At the moment, for example, I was having a very difficult time pulling my attention from his face. The thick lashes and warm brown eyes. How the slope of his nose leaned ever-so-slightly in the same direction as his hair, all of it framing his face and hiding the freckle by his ear. The shape of his lips.

We were texting back and forth as we sat side by side, and Riah laughed at what I'd just sent him. That was another thing—his laugh and the tone of his voice.

I didn't know how much longer I could act normal—like we were just friends. Best friends. But I also didn't know how to tell him, after three years, that I wanted more.

Not that it mattered at the moment. It was a bad time, considering I had to be at work in ten minutes. And also, as much as it might be wanting to burst out of me, it would also be terrifying. What if he didn't feel the same? What if it changed everything?

"I don't have time to bring you home," I said, pulling my feet down from his lap.

"I know, I figured you were bringing me to work with you."

I'd done a lot of that lately, whenever he wasn't already working his real job at the town hall. "That was sort of my plan. Wanna?"

"I think it's my most lucrative hobby." He stood and grabbed my keys from the table. "Last Saturday, Mr. P handed me a fifty from the till."

The first time Riah made himself useful at Parrino's, it was because we were all working—me, Ethan, and Stella. He'd come in with his sisters and their friends to eat pizza, but instead of leaving with them, he'd wandered into the kitchen and helped with closing tasks.

The three of us worked pretty much every Saturday night, and when Riah started complaining about having to spend so much time with his sisters, Ethan told him to stop whining and come with us instead. So he did.

Mr. Parrino kept an eye on Riah as he helped Ethan in the kitchen, did the dishes when the dishwasher went on break, slid into the hostess stand when the hostess was dealing with a high maintenance customer, and helped Stella and I deliver drinks and bread when things got crazy.

A few weeks later he did it again, and then again, until it became a regular thing.

We entered in back, directly into the kitchen, where Ethan was being bossed around by his brother. After graduating last year, Eric had become a full-time cook. Being the newest on the schedule, he worked most Saturdays with the rest of us.

I stopped at the time clock and punched in. It was an old mechanical thing that actually punched the time and date with ink. Eric grumbled about it every time it made its satisfying click, since he was the one who had to take it apart and put it back together when it broke down, something that was happening more and more lately.

Stella breezed through the door as I adjusted my black pencil skirt and smoothed my white blouse. She punched in, kissed me on the cheek, and rushed past me into the main part of the restaurant for the hostess stand, pulling her strawberry blonde hair into a bun while she went. I followed her, and we both peered over Sutton's shoulder to find out what section we had.

I scanned the tables on his clipboard and noted with a sinking stomach that I'd finally been assigned to the cellar. Stella, along with Carrie and Robby, had the dining room, and Iris was on pizza duty. Pizza duty was what we called the tables clustered by the front window on the bar side, since the menu there was limited to soup, salad, and pizza.

With a sigh, I wandered over to the booth where Robby was prepping. He was forming cloth napkins into tulips, something I still hadn't mastered, and Stella slid in across from him to pour salt. I slumped down next to her.

"What's the matter, love?" Robby asked without looking up, his tongue sticking out a little in concentration.

"She got the cellar," Stella told him.

"I don't get how you can handle the scampering shrimp but not the blood pies."

"Mmm, scampering shrimp." Stella took the moment to pat her belly in appreciation. The staff called the shrimp scampi scampering shrimp because that was pretty much what it did. It was a tricky plate to get to the table. Live shrimp, after all, were a bit frantic when thrown onto hot garlic butter sauce.

It wasn't the blood itself that turned my stomach. I was used to that by now. It was the smell of it, hot and reheated. The whole cellar had a cloying, metallic scent that hung like a cloud in the air.

Robby looked up, pleased with his napkin creation, and glanced toward the opening that led to the cellar stairs, where Sutton was leading Sofia and Elbie down the steps. I groaned.

Sofia had hated me since the first day of freshman year when I'd unknowingly moved in on her boyfriend. Who later became my boyfriend. Who was now no one's boyfriend. Elbie was a wild who moved to town last year when our new town council opened our borders to any abnormals, not just the pacifists. The two of them were now a thing.

At the bottom of the narrow stone steps was a small room with five tables and a little bar. The lights were low, same as the rest of the restaurant, but the candles sat in red votives on dark wood, rather than the white on white of the upstairs dining room. Constantine, the bloodtender, nodded at me as I approached and grabbed a tray of shots, which was the cellar's first course instead of bread.

Bracing myself, I approached their table and forced a smile. "Good evening."

Sofia let out a surprised laugh, probably in delight that I had to serve her.

I set the shots between them and kept to the script. "A Parrino trio for you to enjoy. The cold one"—Elbie's face twisted in disgust at this—"is polar bear and will cool your body temperature. I've been told it's quite refreshing. The one that's room temp is feline and stirs contentment. The one steaming hot is a special sloth and tortoise mixture that Constantine created just for us. It should relax you." As if they needed that, vampires. They were cool as cool could be. Well, most of them. Maybe not Sofia.

She held the steaming shot glass under her nose and took a deep breath in, then waved me away with the flick of a hand.

"I'll give you a minute to look over the menu," I said, before heading back to Constantine.

Sutton sat another table, and after greeting them, I noticed Sofia put her menu down with what looked like decision. Might as well get it over with.

"Are you ready to order?" I asked as sweetly as I could muster.

She looked up at me with a smile I knew to be fake. "I assume you're not willing to cut your shoulder for me?" Cutting skin allowed a vampire to drink fresh without turning the person into a vampire themselves, which is what happened when their teeth pierced your skin.

"I won't be bleeding for anyone tonight, thank you. Would a big fat head of garlic suffice?" Ingested, garlic was poison to a vampire.

"Hm, no." As if she had to think about it. "But speaking of heads, I'd take yours on a platter."

"The only head I'll be serving tonight is yours. I'm sure someone here would cut it off for me." If a vampire's head was removed from its body for more than a few minutes, the vampire would become a vegetable. "It might be the simplest way for you to get me out of your life."

"Still so soft, I see, that you couldn't even stomach to cut it off yourself."

I sighed. "If there was ever a head I could stomach to cut off, it would be yours."

Elbie let out a short laugh. "You two are funny," he said.

"All right, so any blood pies?" I asked. "Or just a mug of human?"

"One, I suppose."

"Elbie?" I turned to him. "Would you like a mug of human as well?"

"No. I don't do stale nutrients."

I hoped that meant he'd grown accustomed to the blood bank and the dendrites who offered themselves up as live feed, rather than that he was hunting the surrounding towns. Hard to tell anymore, though. The new town council was a bit more lax on that kind of thing than the old one had been. A bit more forgiving of the purists and elitists.

Purists were those who believed we should live by instinct, even if that meant drinking from and tearing apart unsuspecting humans. Elitists believed the above-normals were at the top of the food chain and shouldn't hide, but be out in the open and run the world. And pacifists were happy to hide for the sake of peace between species, either in small communities like Shady Woods, alone among normals, or in the shadows and hollows of society.

Blood pie, please, I told Ethan and Eric with the power of my dendrite mind, while I swung over to grab Sofia's mug from Constantine. After taking another order and greeting a third table with another trio, I ran upstairs to make sure Ethan and Eric had time to register what I'd sent them, since sometimes on Saturday nights they were so busy they couldn't stop to write it down.

I walked in the kitchen to find them sneezing all over each other.

"What are you guys doing?"

Eric snickered. "Dad just kicked Riah out of here."

"He boogered in the carbonara." Ethan fake sneezed directly into Eric's face.

"That's disgusting. Did you have to dump it?"

"He didn't actually sneeze in it," Noah, the other cook on duty, replied. "He was over by the dirty dishes. Mr. P's just real freaky about his kitchen being clean and germ free."

"I don't think fake sneezing is clean and germ free," I muttered. "Don't you guys have work to do?"

"Please, all we got so far were your two blood pies and a vodka cream sauce."

"Ooh, vodka cream sauce." The whole kitchen said it with me, even Jack who was stationed by the dishwasher. "Yum," I finished, as I generally did when I heard it mentioned.

Stella breezed in and threw four tables worth of orders on the counter. "Get to work, boys!" she sang.

I ducked out the door, checked on my tables, and came back up to find Riah sitting at the end of the bar, near the stairs. He was playing with the napkin his soda sat on.

Letting myself get close enough that my hip rested against his knee, I said, "I heard you sneezed in the carbonara."

"I did not sneeze in the carbonara. I sneezed in the dirty dishes. Which, might I add, were already dirty."

"Same difference," I said, wanting to reach out and touch him.

"I'm not sick," he insisted.

He'd been sick for a few weeks now, which had come at quite the convenient time for me. "You sound sick. Like your nose is stuffed up."

"My nose is fine."

"What am I feeling then?" I held my breath, hoping he wouldn't get it right. He could smell emotions like any good werewolf so I was playing with fire here.

Without breaking eye contact, he reached out for my waist to pull me closer. My body slid up next to his, between his legs, and he rested his nose in my hair.

Normally, he only needed one deep breath to decipher my emotions, but he drew in three long and steady inhales.

The exhales tickled. I shivered as he let go and relaxed back into his seat. Grumbling something, he gazed into his soda.

I smiled, surely seductively, though I wasn't aiming for it. I didn't think I could help how I smiled at him these days. "You're kind of cute when you pout."

"Why are you looking at me like that?"

"Like what?"

"Like that! Have you always looked at me like that, and I never noticed because I knew all I needed by smelling you? Or is this a new look?"

"I don't know. What kind of look is it?" Because if he was seeing what I thought he was seeing, then he didn't need his nose, he was doing just fine without it.

"It's like you..." He ducked his head. "Never mind."

I studied his face, trying to decide if the 'never mind' was due to frustration or avoidance. Frustration because he couldn't smell me, or avoidance because he could, and he didn't want to ruin a good thing. Our friendship being the good thing. The best.

"You're sick. It'll be over soon."

"But what do you smell like?"

I bit my lip as my heart pounded at the cataclysmic change that would take place if I ever did let these particular feelings out. Plus, I was at work. "I guess you'll have to wait to find out."

Heading back to the kitchen, I blew him a kiss, a weak shadow of what I really wanted, and told myself I'd wait until he could smell again. Then he'd know, right? And I wouldn't have to tell him.

The ball would be in his court.

Chapter Two

Did He Hit On You?

Stella and Aster stood at the entrance to the lunchroom. They were staring at someone, but not the table of wilds who'd decided to try their hand at high school this year, which was who I usually kept an eye on.

"Did you see him yet?" Aster asked.

"Who?"

"The new kid."

"Like, an actual new kid? Not a wild new kid?" I lined up next to them, now scanning for someone I didn't recognize. There—a blond with a chiseled, scowling face. Did scowls work so well for everyone or was it just him?

"I don't think I can look away," Aster muttered. "He's gorgeous."

"I don't think I can look at him at all," Stella said. "He's so hot it *hurts* to look at him."

I snorted a little. "You *are* looking at him."

"He is so what I need right now," Aster decided. "I'm going to ask him to sit with us."

She veered off in his direction and I headed to our table. Stella looked between us, then followed Aster. It didn't take too long before the three of them joined us.

"This is Nathan." Aster nudged everyone down a seat until there were two spots between me and Stella, where Aster normally sat. Nathan took the one next to me.

"He's Mr. Jameson's son," she said. Mr. Jameson was Mr. Turner's replacement and had just started that morning. "Nathan, this is Grace, Riah, Jeremy, Christian, and Ethan."

"Nice to meet you." He spoke with a soft Southern drawl.

Aster positively curled at the sound while I said hello and the boys nodded. Jeremy frowned at Aster, which both Stella and I caught, and Stella raised an eyebrow at me.

"Where're you from, Nathan?" Ethan asked.

He shrugged. "We've lived in a bunch of abnormal towns—"

"A bunch?" I coughed over my bite of apple. "I didn't know there were a bunch."

"Plenty. And we've lived in normal communities too." He leaned a little too close in my direction. "Bet you haven't known anyone who's lived normal."

"Actually, she herself has lived normal," Riah clipped. Grabbing my chair, he yanked me closer to him. Werewolves were strong like that.

And now it was Christian who was raising an eyebrow.

"I grew up in Chicago," I told him, ignoring whatever commentary my ex-boyfriend was trying to impart.

"Where've you lived? Normal wise?" Aster asked.

"Where've you lived, *abnormal* wise?" I countered.

Nathan looked between us and picked me. "Lincoln, Colorado. Oasis, Florida. And Minassah, Maine."

I was impressed. Pretty sure it showed on my face, because Nathan seemed pleased to have impressed me.

"There's more than that," Riah mumbled, biting into his sandwich with an attitude.

"Really?" I asked.

"Yes, really. And probably even more we don't know of."

"Huh." I sat back in my chair.

"Normal wise," Nathan turned to Aster, "I've lived in Houston, Texas. Alpharetta, Georgia. Bisbee, Arizona," he glanced over at me with a smile, "and Okay, Oklahoma."

"You're dendrite?" I guessed. Seeing as his dad was teaching dendrite skills.

"And human."

I blinked. "Your mom is normal?"

He smirked. "That's how it would work."

"Is she *here*?" I mean, why not? If wilds could adapt to living in Shady, why not a normal as well?

"No." His face clouded over. "She's been gone a long time."

Oh. That shook me out of my curiosity long enough to notice

that Aster was scolding me with her face. Which meant I was being nosy and hogging the new kid, who she clearly wanted to hog. Stuffing my mouth, I motioned for her to take over, and the conversation began again. I was careful to be a good listener this time.

My curiosity was not tamped down, however, and I slumped into my seat in English with the nagging feeling that he reminded me of someone. As if my thoughts could summon him, which they couldn't—they could do a lot but not that—he appeared in front of me.

"This seat taken?" he asked.

"Yes, actually."

He sat down anyway. *My turn to ask you some questions.*

I narrowed my eyes. It was not cool to break into someone's head like that. There was common courtesy to invading a mind, the first step of which was getting to know them and establishing a bit of trust.

You have a boyfriend?

I only stared at him as Nora walked up. It was her seat he'd taken, not that she seemed to mind. She was nearly drooling.

"Nora, Nathan, Nathan, Nora."

He nodded at her quickly before turning back to me. *Well?*

I shifted uncomfortably in my seat, sort of wishing Riah were here to yank my desk closer to him. Not that I needed to be claimed, but I wouldn't mind an excuse to tuck myself under Riah's arm anyway.

Sofia, of all people, saved me. She stalked up, stood between us, and held out a hand like she expected him to kiss it. "I'm Sofia."

"Nathan." But he ignored her hand.

Tucking it to her side, she crossed her arms and turned to me. "I don't trust him, for the record."

I raised an eyebrow at her and she smiled sweetly, then went to take her seat. Was this because Aster had already mentioned him to her, and she was feeling protective? Or had she thought he was harassing me and was trying to help me out of it? We weren't friends, but we'd worked together before.

I'm not into werewolves, Nathan muttered in my head, drawing my attention back to his. *But I do have a thing for dendrites.*

Kindly get out of my head.

He only smirked, then turned said smirk up to Nora, who was still standing there like a deer in headlights. Patting his lap for her to sit on it, he winked.

Gross, I told him.

"Nora." Mr. Jacobsen motioned to the empty seat on the other side of the room as the bell rang.

After class, I hurried to my locker, thankful Nathan and his dad hadn't shown up at the beginning of the year. Being that we were well underway, the lockers had already been assigned. Otherwise, his Jameson would have ended up right next to my James.

That was the last thing I needed, if he was going to be all pushy.

Riah sauntered over and tilted his head at me. "What are you frowning about?"

"Nathan." I shut my locker and we headed to psych.

"Do you like him?"

"Since when does a frown imply liking something?"

"Did he hit on you?"

I glanced over, trying to read his expression.

"He was looking at you at lunch," he explained. "I didn't like it."

"You didn't?"

He eyed me. "What happened in English? Did he hit on you? Do you like him?"

"Riah, I just told you I don't like him."

"I know, but sometimes girls say that and don't mean it."

"Who do you believe then? The girl or yourself?"

Looking away, he replied, "I always believe the girl."

"That doesn't make sense, Riah. Your nose doesn't lie."

He shrugged. "Sometimes people lie to themselves. It's not for me to point that out."

As we entered the room, I looked around to make sure psych wasn't also an elective that Nathan had chosen. "It doesn't matter if he hit on me. I do not like him."

"So he *did* hit on you."

"He asked me if I had a boyfriend. I might need you to pretend you're my boyfriend."

He didn't reply, almost like I hadn't said anything at all. Right. Not into it. But before I went to sit down, he slipped his hand in mine. "It wouldn't be so hard to pretend."

Someone squeezed past me, and I took a step into Riah. He was a little taller than me, but not much, and our chests were nearly touching. I should move back. There was room to move back or sit down, but I didn't want to.

"What do you think that would entail?" I asked softly, tilting my head up to his.

"It was your idea. You tell me."

"Like, ground rules?"

"Sure. Ground rules. Or what you'd want me to do if we were pretending. Would we have to kiss?"

The bell rang, and as it pulled my focus away from him, I realized the entire class was watching us, along with Ms. Clawson.

Have to sounded like he didn't want to. He could've just said, "Would we kiss?" and left it at that. On the other hand, the way he'd said, "It wouldn't be so hard to pretend" with his serious voice, the one that had weight and depth and a certain softness to it, made me think he might enjoy it, pretending. Plus, he hadn't wasted any time taking my hand.

It occurred to me that he hadn't dated anyone since he broke up with Kiara last year, shortly after I'd broken up with Christian. And he hardly spent time with anyone besides me, Stella, and Ethan. I guess Aster was with us a lot. Maybe he was into her. Probably, actually. Everyone was into her.

Siren skills for the non-siren was my last class of the day. It was a senior elective almost everyone took, including all the wild vampires who'd decided to try out high school. They didn't need to take vampires skills to learn sonar mapping and what animal bloods could do for them, because they'd lived it. The wild werewolves, on the other hand, *were* taking wolf skills, because no one had taught them how to pull out a non-emotive aroma or how to differentiate between the scent of emotions and illnesses.

The siren skills room was set up like our chem lab. Aster and I had the counter behind Ethan and Riah, which was in front of Christian and Jeremy.

Nathan walked up. "Hey, Grace." He nodded at me and no one else.

I opened my mouth but didn't reply because I was too busy trying to figure out how to pretend that Riah and I were dating, when we were surrounded by all our friends who knew very well that we weren't.

"Hi Nathan," Aster replied, elbowing me like I was the rude one. I rolled my eyes to her. He was most definitely the rude one.

Without answering, he squeezed around Aster to settle between us.

With a frown, I pulled the flask of fresh siren tears toward me, ready to make some fancy household cleaning solution as soon as Ms. Zieir gave us the green light.

Tell me about yourself, Nathan said, once her short lecture was over. As if he thought we could have some cute, private, flirtatious conversation while the world continued on, oblivious, around us. Which was rude. And also, no.

I asked you to stay out of my head, I reminded him.

You asked me to get *out of your head.* His arm brushed mine as he passed things back and forth between Aster and I, which was about all he contributed to the process.

Well, now I'm asking you to stay out.

The corner of his lip curled up, as if I was only a challenge that entertained him, and after a few minutes, he turned to Aster. She smiled sweetly and proceeded to answer every question he posed to her, about who was with who and what kinds of things people did around here.

Nathan didn't ask her directly if I was with anyone, or if Riah was, so I decided we'd make a plan that afternoon. We'd have to convince our friends, as well, because there were too many people to let in on the secret. Would they buy it? It could be like a test run.

When the bell rang, I skirted the counter to block Riah from getting out. *Can we talk tonight?*

He ducked his head to mine. "About how Nathan clearly has a thing for you?"

"And Aster clearly has a thing for Nathan?"

"And how it would make things easier if you were off the table?"

I frowned, caught between how this phrasing implied I was something available for the taking and the fact that I indeed wanted him to take me off the table. "Think we could do it?" I asked, pulling back to look at him now that the room was almost empty.

His gaze didn't waver from mine when he said, "Take you off the table?"

My heart palpitated in my chest. It was clearly not getting the message that we were talking about pretending. I nodded and he grinned.

"I'll come over right after work."

Chapter Three

Slim to None

When the doorbell rang before dinner, it wasn't Riah I found on the front porch, but the new kid. And his father.

A smirk grew across Nathan's face as I tried to wrap my mind around what they could possibly be doing at my house. If he hadn't given me creep vibes before, he definitely did with that particular smile.

Mr. Jameson set a hand on Nathan's shoulder and peered past me into the house. It felt invasive, so I stepped in his way and blocked his view.

"Can I help you?" I asked.

This teacher of mine looked as bewildered as I felt. "Is your dad home?"

My eyes swept from him to his son as I called, *Dad? Someone's here for you.*

My mom wandered in from the living room. I heard her footsteps and then her gasp. "Richard?"

"Anna." Striding past me, Mr. Jameson held his arms open and my mother sunk into him, like they went way back.

They couldn't go way back. I'd gone through a phase where I pored over all their pictures from their entire lives, obsessed with the idea that my parents existed before me, and he wasn't in any of them.

My dad stumbled down the last few steps of the stairs, his face drained of color like he'd seen a ghost. But when Mr. Jameson let go of my mom, they embraced, slapping each other on the back. My dad grinned. "Wow."

"Wow is right," my new teacher said, holding my dad for an uncomfortably long time. He even went so far as to clasp my dad's face as they pulled away.

My dad shook his head. "Where've you been? And what are the odds we'd both end up back here?"

"Slim to none, I'd have said," Mr. Jameson replied with a grin, gripping my dad in another hug.

Mom. What is happening right now?

"Come in, Nate," my mom said, as if she knew him too. "We're about to have dinner. You must stay." After closing the door behind him, she pulled a piece of lint off his shirt and adjusted his collar, fluttering about him like he was her own.

Mom.

Instead of answering me, she clasped her hands together and said, "I'll go set two more places at the table."

Mr. Jameson turned to me. "Grace James." He shook his head. "You threw me for a loop when I walked into class today."

We stared at each other uncomfortably, after which he threw his arms open for a hug.

Um, no.

I spun on a heel and crossed my arms when I reached the kitchen. My teacher slipped past me, exclaimed over my brother, who was dressing a salad, and asked my mom if he could help. When she insisted he sit, he approached me, shaking his head again.

"I thought, 'James? Is this why I haven't had any luck finding them?'"

"Ah, well. Cutting ties, Rich. I needed to cut ties." My dad sat down as Justin and Clara brought over the serving dishes.

"Can't blame you there, brother."

Brother? I broke into my mom's head. My dad wasn't the type to call people "brother," and also, he didn't have one.

She motioned for me to take my seat. "I think maybe the kids are a little confused."

My dad glanced between me and Justin with a proud smile. "Say hello to your uncle, kids. And your cousin, Nate."

I blinked at them. At my parents, trying to gauge if they were serious. At my...uncle? And my...Nate. Nathan. Who was watching me, still with that smirk. My first thought was that him being my cousin at least took care of one problem. My second? That I no longer needed to pretend anything with Riah, which was something I'd really been looking forward to.

Justin clasped hands with Nathan, as if this was all it took to welcome someone into your family.

My brother was infuriating. He took everything in stride.

"You're an only child," I reminded my dad.

"We lost touch after your grandpa died," he replied.

I emphasized my previous statement about him *telling us he was an only child* with a violent shake of my head and a throwing of my hands in the air. How had this never come up?

"After your grandpa died, we legally changed our name," my mom explained. "You were born Grace Jameson."

"Justin Jameson has a nice ring to it." My brother squeezed Clara's hand.

"When did grandpa die?" I asked my dad.

"You were three."

I turned to my brother, who was a few years older than me. "You don't remember any of this?"

He shrugged. "I remember a funeral."

"Let's not talk about this now," my dad said, giving me a sharp look. "I'd like to catch up with my brother, who I haven't seen in fourteen years."

I gave him a sharp look right back and turned under the archway. "I'm going to need a minute."

Because *what?* My last name wasn't my last name and my dad had a whole living family he'd lied about? I went out back and paced the square cement patio, trying to calm the anxiety rising up from my toes. Anxiety about what, though? About how the last time something this big shook my life, I'd had to leave everything behind and move to Shady Woods? That had turned out all right. This would too. If anything, maybe having long-lost family here would keep my parents from any more discussions about the state of Shady, how it wasn't strictly pacifist any longer, and how maybe we should move back normal.

This wasn't a big deal, I told myself. It was just an uncle and a cousin. Many people had uncles and cousins.

But if it were that simple, why were there no pictures of them anywhere? And why would we change our name?

I slumped down into a patio chair as my mom stepped outside with a plate. She set it on the table and scooted it closer to me with the push of one finger. "Your current attitude leaves much to be desired."

My current attitude? The one resulting from being lied to?

With a pout, I stared at the bowl of chicken and dumplings. Maybe they were planning on answering questions and explaining themselves tomorrow. Maybe tonight, they just wanted a happy reunion. Even so, I couldn't bring myself to go back inside. My current "attitude" wasn't going anywhere, so honestly, they should be glad I was out here.

I wanted my phone, wanted to text Riah and Stella and Aster, but it was on the kitchen counter and I couldn't bring myself to go in for it. The windows were closed but I could hear their laughter. Their cooing. Their general getting reacquainted.

It was obvious everyone in that kitchen was delighted. Not me. I wasn't delighted. I was searching through past memories for clues. Through my soul for why I was struggling so much when my brother wasn't. Why I always struggled so much when my brother didn't.

When the dishes started clinking in the sink, the screen door stirred and Nathan sat down next to me. He nodded toward my now cold plate. "You gonna' eat that?"

"Did you know about us?"

He didn't answer, but pulled my plate closer to his side of the table.

"This doesn't bother you?" I pressed.

"It's only bothering you because you had the hots for me," he replied around a mouthful of chicken and dumplings.

I made a face. "You wish."

"I did. I did wish." He laughed and nodded. "I was drawn to you right away. Thought maybe it was the connection of us both having lived normal. Guess it's that we're related."

"Gross," I muttered.

He polished off my plate and set it back down. "It did seem strange, seeing as how you're not very light and fluffy. That's what I usually go for. It's a good counter to me being dark and mysterious."

"I was light and fluffy three years ago," I replied absently, remembering all the things since the move that had little by little plucked the light and fluffy out of me. Not that I was complaining. In this world, I valued fortitude.

"I've never been light and fluffy."

With a sigh, I studied him.

Unconcerned, he leaned back in his chair. "I prefer living normal, but I guess having family around won't be so bad."

As small as Shady felt a lot of the time, living normal was akin to being kept in a box, powered down and frustrated. "You prefer living normal? Really?"

"When I was little, when I wasn't sure if I was going to end up normal or dendrite, I paid attention to everything. I'd spend some days pretending to be one and the next pretending to be the other, so I'd be ready however it ended up."

As he delivered this, I softened. "That must have been hard."

"Must have been?" He raised an eyebrow. "It wasn't hard for you?"

"Why would it be hard for me? My mom's not normal."

"But grandpa was."

I stared at him and gripped the arms of my chair tight. As Nathan realized this was a revelation for me, his eyebrows rose.

And now I was wondering if the whole bit about me revealing my true nature to the wrong person and putting us all in danger had been a lie too. If really it had been that they were waiting to make sure I did, indeed, show dendrite traits before moving us to Shady. I'd thought my parents were honest, truthful, straight-forward people, but if they weren't that, what about my life was actually true?

I leaned forward. "Tell me more."

"Tell you more about what?"

"Tell me everything you know about this family, and start from the beginning."

The sky was halfway to dark, blanketing us in shadow, and the light clicked on by the back door.

"I know Grandma and Grandpa met in Green Bay. Grandma

was dendrite, but taught to hide it, of course—"

"*Master it, hide it, keep it,*" I recited.

"And she did, successfully, until she was in labor the first time. Grandpa put all the other little weird things together and about lost his mind when she told him the truth."

"Nathan," Mr. Jameson called through the screen door. "Time to go."

He stood. "I'll tell you the rest tomorrow."

I grabbed for his hand, like he was the truth and it was slipping away. "Can't you just... tell him you'll come home later? I'll drive you."

A sleazy grin spread across his face. "You do like me, then."

"Ugh." Letting go of him, I rubbed my palm on my jeans, as if touching him had contaminated me.

His grin split into a laugh, relaxing his face into something genuine. "Lunch tomorrow, okay?"

I followed him down the hallway that ran from the backyard to the front foyer, and as my dad closed the door behind them, I turned on my parents to give them one last chance to come clean.

"I'm part normal? Is there anything else you want to tell me?"

"We're part normal?" Justin called from the kitchen sink, where he was finishing up the rest of the dishes with Clara.

"Grandpa was normal," I told him, as he appeared in the archway, drying a pan. He glanced at my mom, who was leaning against the wall there. She didn't deny it.

"Cool," he said, before disappearing again.

I turned back to my dad. "Well?"

"It's not important, Grace. None of that is important."

"None of what is important? What else haven't you told us?"

"My life is not your concern," he snapped, voice tight. "Your life is your concern. You've been safe and loved and cared for. That's what matters." And he marched up the stairs.

I blinked after him.

My dad did not lose his temper. He did not have secrets and problems and demons. But that was a temper I'd just seen. And it had come riding in on a demon.

"Nothing's changed, Grace," my mom said. "I don't know why you think anything has changed."

"He's kept my identity from me! Part normal?! That's like finding out I'm part vampire! Or part wolf! My kids could come out that way! And he's kept family from me! He's a liar!"

"That's enough! You do not call your father a liar. He has not disclosed his life story to you but he is not a liar." And she stalked up the stairs after my dad.

Storming up after them, so they knew I wouldn't be that easy to quiet, I tore into my room for running clothes. Once changed, I marched back downstairs to swing open the door.

Riah was heading up the steps. He scanned me. "Why are you in running clothes?"

"I need to run." I pushed past him, hurrying to my car.

"I thought we were going to talk," he called after me.

"There's nothing to talk about anymore," I said, motioning for him to get in. We ran in the woods behind his house, so whether or not he was coming with me, I was heading there.

"We could walk, maybe?" he asked as he joined me in the car.

"Riah, I'm freaking out. We're running." I peeled out of the driveway.

"Did I miss something?"

"My dad has been lying to me my whole life. It's like I don't even know him anymore. And you should have seen him when I called him on it, he got all snippy with me. Who even is he? And why does my stupid brother not care?"

"Because you're overreacting?"

"You don't even know what I'm talking about." I whipped the car around the corner.

"Then tell me."

"Justin never cared that we were abnormal, he thought it made us special—"

"It does make you special," he broke in softly.

"But I did! I cared! It scared the crap out of me, that I was going to get these abilities and none of my friends were! And to know I had a cousin who understood that? Who understood that maybe we were going to end up normal? I mean, I didn't even know that was a possibility, but had I known, it would have been nice to have someone to talk to. We were both worrying about the same sort of thing, and we could have been worrying together. But instead, we were alone! I had no one! And I could have. He kept that from me. All of that!"

"Whoa, back up."

The car came to a screeching halt in his driveway. I yanked the keys out of the ignition and turned to him, seething all over again.

"I felt alone my entire life—"

"Until you moved here."

"I felt *so alone*. Do you know what that's like? Not having anyone who gets you? You don't. You had everyone. I had Justin, who never cared or worried about anything, and my parents, who didn't grow up normal. I was alone. And Nathan, the one person who might have understood that, who, come to find, *does* understand that, was kept from me."

"Nathan's your cousin? Is that what I'm supposed to be getting from this?"

"And Mr. Jameson's my uncle." I threw open the car door, and when we met back up in the driveway, I stopped to grab his arm. "Riah, my last name is Jameson. My dad changed our name when I was three. I'm not even a James. There *is* no James."

His forehead screwed up in confusion.

"Exactly." I swept through his house to the backyard while he ran upstairs to change.

When he joined me to stretch, he settled down so his left knee touched my right, and that helped. My energy zeroed in where our skin met and I remembered myself, and how much I felt for him, and how I was a somewhat normal girl living a somewhat normal life.

"Why'd he change your name?"

"To cut ties, he said. Whatever that means. And because of that, my uncle couldn't find us. Then my uncle was moving all the time, which made it hard for my dad to find *him*."

"So it's not like he wanted to lose touch, not like he wanted to keep them from you, right?"

I scowled. "Then what ties was he cutting?"

We were quiet while we finished stretching, then Riah stood and offered me both hands. I slid my palms into his and he pulled me up. His wolf strength always overdid it a little so I often tumbled into him, which was my favorite part.

"Are you mad because of what you found out," he asked, "or because your dad didn't answer more questions?"

"How do you know I had more questions?"

He smiled. "You always have more questions."

"Both," I decided, before taking off in a jog. The path through the forest was too narrow for us to run side by side, and I always led, because I could hear him better when we were talking if he was behind me.

Not that I wanted to talk. I wanted to run my frustration out in the dark woods and then practice kissing my pretend boyfriend under the moon in what we now considered our clearing.

But there would be no kissing, because there was no longer any need for a pretend boyfriend. And I wasn't in the right headspace to tell him I wanted the real thing. Not now, and maybe not ever.

Chapter Four

Because I'm Family

It was difficult to pay attention in calc the next day, with my uncle smiling so much in my direction.

I had an uncle. And a cousin. My dad had a *family*, and I could have been normal. I'd thought it was bad enough that I was into my best friend due to the problems that could cause if he didn't feel the same way, particularly since we were planning on going to the same college next year.

It wasn't common for Shady residents to leave, so I guess the fact that he'd applied to UW Madison early decision might have more to do with me than anything else, now that I thought about it.

"Why'd you decide to leave Shady for college?" I asked, meeting up with him at our lockers before lunch.

"Seemed like a good idea to see how normals live." He shrugged. "I thought it might give me some ideas for what we could do here to correct things." He wanted in on that town council, wanted to run things some day, since he no longer trusted anyone else to run them right.

I studied him for a moment. It sounded like a valid enough reason. And had nothing to do with me. I opened my locker and swapped my stuff out. "Normals can be just as corrupt as the new council."

He glanced around as if someone might have heard me, but surely it would come as no surprise that not everyone was on their side. Then his eyes widened. "I can smell your impatience."

"Yeah, well." I was impatient. In general. But also, it was lunch, and that meant more information from Nathan about my family's buried secrets.

His lip tugged up and he hung a hand on the top of his locker door, all cocky. "I can *smell your impatience*." He took a deep breath in, his face breaking out into an amazing smile. "I can smell it."

Uh oh. That meant... "You're not sick anymore?"

He leaned in. "It's okay. I wouldn't have expected you to notice. You've been a little preoccupied."

Shit. Did I send off madly-in-love-with-my-best-friend even though I was consumed with my dad's life story? I was willing to bet I did. He closed his locker and started walking, but now I was frozen.

"Are you coming?" he asked, so cocky with his confidence

back, with his nose feeding him private information about me.

How come I didn't have private information about him? How was that fair?

I followed him, watching his wide shoulders from behind and trying to calm my heart at the small smile he tossed when he glanced back.

With a raised eyebrow, he stopped to wait. "What are you doing?"

I was trying to stay far enough behind that he couldn't smell me, not that I knew how far that would actually be. If he could smell me, why wasn't he saying anything about how I felt?

I hurried past him and nearly ran to the cafeteria. With a deep frown, I gripped the back of Nathan's chair to steady myself as Riah sat down, clearly pleased, which meant he liked me too, right? He wouldn't be smug if he'd realized I'd fallen for him and he didn't feel the same way, would he? That would be cruel. He was not cruel.

When I didn't sit down right away, Nathan stood up into me and tilted his head toward the parking lot. "Let's get out of here."

"She's going to tell us all anyway," Aster said, which was true. But also, I wasn't sure I could focus on Nathan while that grin was on Riah's face. What did it mean, exactly?

"We've already gotten a rundown of last night," Stella added.

Nathan grabbed my lunch bag. "This isn't fairies and roses, Grace."

With a nod, I led him out to the parking lot and unlocked my car.

Sliding into the passenger seat, he opened my lunch bag and went for the grapes, holding them out to offer me some. I shook my head, not sure I could eat anyway.

Was that because of this story I was about to hear, or because Riah had his nose back? I fiddled with my keys and stared at the school stretched out in front of us. "So when Grandpa found out...?"

"She told him it didn't matter. That they could turn out like him. But when Rich started showing ability—"

"You call your dad Rich?"

"She wanted him to go to school here. Grandpa refused to get anywhere near town—"

"Did it change how he felt about them?"

He rolled his eyes to me. "I didn't watch the movie, Grace. I only know the basics."

With a wave of my hand, I motioned for him to go on.

"They got a house about an hour between Shady and Marinette. Grandma could drive them in for school and Grandpa could pretend none of it existed. Then she died. Grandpa wanted to pull the three of them from school but they refused—"

"Three of them?"

"There was a sister."

"Was?"

He pulled my granola bar out of the bag and offered it to me. I shook my head and he tore it open. "Yes. Was."

"She died too?"

"From a broken heart."

I snorted. "No. She did not die from a broken heart. When? When did this supposedly happen?"

"She'd grown up here and all her friends were here, but when her abilities never showed, Grandpa stopped letting her see anyone. She refused to go to school in Marinette and he refused to let her come to Shady, so she spent her days at home alone. One night, they came home and she was dead. Grandpa buried her and called her in as a runaway a few weeks later to avoid an autopsy. Just in case her brain might show something and give any of them away."

I turned to gape at him. *What kind of dead?*

Nate pulled his attention away from my granola bar long enough to snort. *Are there multiple kinds of dead?*

You know what I mean. What happened to her?

A broken heart is what Rich always says. Maybe she had some freak kid heart attack. I don't know. All I know is that grandpa already blamed them for being abnormal in the first place. But then, when he had to hide Grace's body—his eyes shot over to me as I absorbed the impact of her name—*he blamed them for her death as well. For having to keep it secret to protect them. Grandma wasn't around to blame I guess, so he took it out on them.*

I slumped back in my seat. My dad lost a mom and a sister before he graduated high school. He'd then walked away from his dad and brother, purging his belongings of any sign of them. I'd checked the attic and the basement last night after they went to bed, and I was planning to search my parents' room the next time no one was home. Yet still, after all that, he'd named me after her.

I was the memory. I was what he carried around with him.

It was a miserable, abusive few years, the way Rich tells it, and as soon as they were done with school, they took off. Didn't want to be anywhere near him. Or the memories, probably. Nathan trailed a finger along the edge of my sandwich.

"Eat it," I told him, almost sick.

As he finished my lunch, I wondered if it made more sense for our grandma to have raised them all here or my dad to have raised us normal. Either way, the normal child would know the abnormal existed—they had to, they lived with it. Justin and I had always known about Shady, even before Justin showed any signs. We visited my mom's parents every Christmas, and my parents never hid their abilities from us. Would it have been harder for me to have been raised in Shady, only to turn out normal and have to adjust to Chicago, instead of the other way around?

So, this Aster girl, Nathan broke into my thoughts. *What angle should I work with her?*

"What?"

Does she like dark and brooding, romantic and sappy, bored and indifferent? What?

"Why would I tell you that?" Aside from the fact that she liked him and I wanted her to be happy, I was willing to bet he'd be a terrible boyfriend.

He grinned. *Because I'm family.*

"Stop smiling at me like that."

He smiled even more lewdly, something I wouldn't have thought possible. *I'll go romantic and sappy then.*

I frowned. *Her last serious boyfriend was bored and indifferent.* Admitting this was a gamble, but Kevin had also been pretty devoted. Plus, Aster had declared she was over bored and indifferent. Hopefully this was true and it would backfire on him. At least until I had more time to decide for myself if he was the asshat he seemed to be.

He swung my car door open. "Let's go ask her out."

"What?" I scrambled after him, catching up with his long strides as he pushed the double doors to the lunchroom open. "Is something wrong with you?" One second he's telling me about our dead aunt and the next he's ready to snap back to regular high school drama?

"Plenty is wrong with me." He winked as he pushed through Christian and Maribel, who were leaning away from their respective tables to talk to each other.

"Sorry about him," I muttered, squeezing through and stopping abruptly behind Nathan when he didn't sit down.

Crossing his arms and flipping his hair off his forehead, he muttered, "Show me around after school, huh?"

Aster blinked her dark brown eyes up at him. "Me?"

"Sure."

A grin bloomed on her face. "Of course." And she turned back to the remnants of her meat pie, smug.

"Ugh." I shoved him out of the way and asked her, "Can I talk to you for a second?"

She sighed. "Must you?"

"Yes."

Stella wafted some charm over both of us. I could tell because Aster cut her the same sharp look I did. Sometimes I loved how siren charm could make me feel better, but sometimes I preferred to arm myself with my irritation. This was one of those times, so I did my best to counter it.

Pushing her seat back, Aster led me out of the lunchroom.

"What are you thinking?" I hissed as I followed her. "He's not worth your time."

At my locker, she spun to face me and put her hands on her hips. "Every boy in this school is too intimidated by me or too easily intimidated in general." She *was* intimidating. If there was one person who had their crap together in this town, it was Aster Stickman. And she could smell people's fear of her, being she was a wolf, which was apparently pretty noxious.

"Jeremy isn't," I pointed out. And, come to think of it, he seemed to be frowning a lot lately, in direct proportion to how often she smiled at Nathan.

She waved the idea of Jeremy away as if he were irrelevant. "Nathan defers to no one but his father, which is kind of adorable. And now that he knows you two are related, he wants me. He can try to hide it behind whatever game he's playing, but he can't fool my nose. Anyway, do you not think I, of all people, can take care of myself?"

She could smell him. She could smell that he wanted her. I ran a hand across my face. "Shit."

"Honestly, Grace, do you not think I can take care of myself? I'm a *werewolf*."

"Not shit *you*, shit Riah."

"Shit Riah what?"

"He's not sick anymore."

"Yeah, so?"

"So I'm... I like him. And he can smell it. And he's not doing anything about it. So he doesn't like me, right? You must be able to smell how he feels."

"Everyone can smell how he feels," she muttered. "Why do you think Christian was such a pain in your ass?"

"What are you talking about? Christian can't smell anything." It was his portent dreams that were a pain in my ass.

Her face softened and we were us again. "Oh, honey. He didn't have to be able to smell it."

"What are you saying?"

She cleared her throat. "You know I'm not supposed to say anything."

I nodded. It wouldn't be very nice if wolves went around announcing everyone's deepest, darkest emotions. "But you're my best friend."

"Riah's your best friend," she corrected.

"That's exactly what I'm worried about." I started pacing. "He must not want to take this any further. Which I get. It'll probably ruin everything."

"You realize you've smelled the same as him for a very long time, right?"

"What do you mean?"

"You've smelled like you liked him for years and never acted on it. So of course he's not going to do anything now. To him, it's all the same. Just because you finally woke up doesn't mean he can tell that difference. He doesn't trust himself anymore. You're going to have to lead this one."

My brain spun through all the times he'd asked me what I was thinking, even though he could smell what I was feeling, and my throat went dry. "You're not wrong," I said, only just now realizing it.

"Please, girl, when am I wrong?"

"Aster..." I stared at her. Terrified. "I don't know if I can do it. What if he doesn't like me?"

"Oh, he likes you."

"Okay, but what if he doesn't think it's a good idea?"

"Everyone thinks it's a good idea."

"But what if it screws everything up?"

"That's the gamble with life, babe. Every decision and every day. You've just got to jump."

Chapter Five

It Was a Joint Effort

As the minutes ticked by that afternoon, everything Riah had ever said that could have hinted at how he felt floated into my consciousness, and as this accumulated a mountain of proof I'd never before acknowledged, I grew more and more anxious. Needless to say, I was jittery as I drove us to his house after school.

We were quiet in the car, but the chemistry between us was loud. Hot, too. It was a sixty-degree October day, but I had to roll the windows down and turn on the air to be comfortable.

Then my brain would spin and I'd be back to doubting, feeling like maybe Aster was just trying to get back at me for being a turd about her and Nathan. But that wasn't Aster. She loved me, and she kind of even loved Riah. She wouldn't do that. Yet, when you wanted something so badly, but were scared of what you might lose in the process of trying to get it, it was nearly impossible to talk yourself over the fear.

Or that's where I seemed to be anyway.

I parked on the street, turned off the car, and looked at my best friend. Is this how he'd felt for... how long? And I'd just been over here, blissfully ignorant and tormenting him every day?

How awful.

He turned to me. "All right. What's going on?"

I choked on my answer and got out of the car.

Catching up to me on the porch, he followed me through his house, where I tossed my keys in the kitchen and headed out back into the woods.

"Grace, I don't understand what you smell like right now."

Holding my chest, pressing my palm against the tightness there, I took our path to the clearing. Over the summer, Riah and I had nailed plywood to the trees and built a crude rack that faintly resembled Jeremy's. We'd ridden out to the truck stop to buy a few of Mr. Holmes' axes, and I was pleased to note that Jeremy's dad no longer struck me as creepy, the way he had back when I was embedded in the normal world.

"If you're worried about Aster and Nathan, she can handle herself," he said as I grabbed his axe. The big one. "If he tried anything, she could take him, no contest."

"I'm not worried about Aster." Well, I was. But he was right, as was she. Aster could definitely handle herself. She'd trained me before Jeremy had, who'd trained me before Ethan, who'd trained me before Riah, so I should know how fierce she was, not to mention her wolf strength and natural affinity for stalking and hunting prey.

Stepping closer to me, Riah reached out for my hand and the axe. Prying my fingers from its handle, he set it back in the rack. "Grace, not only can every wolf smell you in a one-mile radius, but your hands are shaking. What are you so scared of?"

"You," I admitted, before I could think too much about it. Forcing myself to meet his eyes, I added. "Us."

"I don't understand."

"I think you do." *Please don't make me say it.*

"Grace, I—"

"Trust yourself, Riah. I know you haven't... not with me... for, I don't know how long, but... but you can now, okay? I'm trying to say..." I had to clear my throat of the emotion there. My palms were sweaty and I was no longer certain of anything. He could smell me, so what was he waiting for? "I'm trying to say I realize it now. I—"

His eyes scanned my face, from my eyes to my lips, and his forehead creased in question. Yes. That's right. That's what I'm talking about. Lips and kisses.

I sighed. *What do I smell like?*

With my words in his head, he looked back up to meet my gaze. "You smell terrified."

What else?

"You smell like you always do."

Which is what?

He blinked.

Tell me.

"But you're terrified."

I nodded. *Do it anyway.*

"Why are you terrified?"

Because I can't lose you. What do I smell like?

"Grace. You can't lose me. You won't."

My head cleared at the softening of his tone, and at his words. "Riah." *What do I smell like?*

Moments. Eyes. Wind in his hair.

"You smell like..."

I waited for him to say it, but when he didn't, I prodded, *Like what?*

"Like..." His Adam's apple bobbed. He shook his head and turned away.

Hand trembling, I put my fingers to his chin and gently coaxed his attention back to me. *Believe it,* I said, dropping my hand from his face, only for him to catch it in his own. My heart pounded its wings against my ribcage, then rocked and struggled and made me feel like I'd never been truly alive before that moment. "What do you smell like?" I asked. "When we're together, what do you smell like?"

His mouth opened but he didn't speak. He only searched my eyes.

I looked to our feet, to the crunchy grass of October between us. "Are you... empty... when I'm not around?" I couldn't look at him now. He'd been on a quest to describe love last year—what it felt like to love someone—and this was the definition he came up with. That when the person you loved wasn't around you felt like a piece of yourself was missing. And when you were with them, you felt content. Full. Satiated. "When we're together, do you feel..."

"Whole," he finished, so softly I couldn't be sure the breeze hadn't said it. "I feel *right* when you're around." He tugged me closer.

We'd been plenty close many times before, but not like this. Not like anything that would have remotely resembled an embrace. And I realized that hugs and cuddling side by side on a couch, working on the same thing, or even being locked tight together at the end of a sparring session, one person on top of the other, none of that was the same as standing face to face, so close the wind couldn't sweep between us. So close I might easily stumble into him, mouth to mouth. And holding that position, our hands linked loosely together, looking into each other's eyes, was intimate in a way we'd never known before, even though we'd shed all our masks and shared all our secrets.

My skin purred with a gentle buzz and I glanced at my fingertips to make sure they weren't actually sending out any electrical impulses.

When I looked back up at him, he muttered, "Okay, maybe now *I'm* terrified."

"Right? What if this screws everything up?"

"And by *this,* you mean... just so I'm sure..."

"I mean..." My eyelids fluttered, my gaze skittering away from his eyes to his lips to the sliver of space between us.

Gah. How was it so impossible to tell him what I wanted, when he was the person I'd been most comfortable with only an hour before?

I let my fingers slip to his waist and and tugged him closer, hoping that would say something, anything, while I tried to search out my courage.

He slid his hand up my arm, trailing it slowly to my chin. As I looked back at him, he ran a course thumb lightly over my lips. "You mean this?"

With a hard swallow, I nodded.

"Are you saying I can kiss you?" he whispered, his forehead touching down on mine.

I'm saying I want you to.

Tilting my chin up, he touched his lips down so lightly on mine that it felt like a whisper or a promise. I responded, tentative. Because even though he'd started it, I still somehow doubted he was in. But soon, between the give and take, a conversation all its own, our kiss deepened with intention and meaning and years of locked down emotion finally making its way to the surface. It felt like my heart was nearly coming unhinged inside my chest with the terror and the thrill and the *want* and the *finally*.

Finally? Had it known all this time? Wrapping my arms tight around Riah's neck, I moved to bury my face against his cheek. "I'm so stupid," I muttered.

He wrapped his arms around me tight and whatever space had been between us before—literally and figuratively—disappeared. "When you say that, you don't mean this is stupid, right? You don't mean *we're* stupid?"

"No. I mean stupid for not seeing earlier." I held him as tight as I held myself, afraid that unbeknownst to me, my emotions might actually be spilling into him of their own accord, since that was something my mind could do.

We might have kissed and he might be able to smell the truth of it, but wanting him was so strong, so pure, so deep a part of me, that it about bowled me over. How could it not send him running, if he actually felt it firsthand himself?

"This is a pretty crap deal for me," I muttered. "You'll always be able to smell exactly how I feel about you, and I'll only ever be able to guess."

He leaned back to look at me and I let him, loosening my arms. "It'll make up for all the time I smelled it while you were dating other people and had to convince myself I was crazy." Setting the tip of his nose on my forehead, he ran it along the edge of my hair, down to my neck. The contact was new and my knees went to rubber. His hands on my waist held me up, and then his mouth took over for his nose, pressing one kiss against my skin. "I was so jealous watching you and Jeremy last year, the way he'd land those kisses on your neck when you were sparring. In front of everyone too."

"You were still with Kiara then," I reminded, astonished at the difference between how I felt when Jeremy did it, to how I felt now. Kiss or no, I'd stiffened under Jeremy, every time. Even after I knew it would be lips instead of teeth. I just hadn't trusted him. But with Riah, were he a vampire, I might just drop my head to the side and let him bite me. My stomach was absolutely putty. I cared about nothing else. I was worried about nothing else. He was currently consuming me.

The smile on his face bloomed something inside my chest, something that unfurled so fast and furiously that it ached. "Because you told me not to break up with her until after the dance," he said.

I laughed, which was a poor choice, because it absolutely broke the magic of the moment. What had felt like a pause in time and place was gone—the woods around us, the wind and birds, they'd been silent and still and now their noise and movement swept back in. Laughing with him, like I had so many times before, but this time in his arms, felt suddenly awkward.

He must have felt me stiffen because he let go of me, a frown tugging down only one side of the lips I'd just had mine on.

We stared at each other. I shook my head.

"Did you just panic?" he asked.

"A little."

"Do you want this?"

"I do." I crossed my arms, completely awkward now. "The amount of times Stella put your name on my list." I rolled my eyes, trying to play normal. "How can I be so smart about so many things and so stupid about this?"

"What's going on right now?"

"That didn't feel awkward to you? Us acting normal while...in an *embrace?*"

"We've arguably embraced before."

"We've never embraced before."

"We touch each other all the time."

Those words paused time and place again.

We stared at each other, hardly breathing. We did touch each other all the time. But now every one of those touches meant something different. Or, at least, we knew what those touches meant now. And when laced with intention, it made them heavier. In a good way, but also...

"Okay, I see it," he said, huffing a short expression of amusement and taking the pressure off once again. "Let's distract ourselves with my sisters. They'll make you feel smarter, too." He offered me his hand and we both looked at it as I took it.

"That's not very nice to say about your sisters," I said, relearning how his fingers felt in mine as we headed back to the house.

"I'm not saying anything about my sisters. I'm saying you're brilliant. And anyway, I'm supposed to say that about my sisters. It keeps them humble."

"What about me? You're no longer keeping me humble?"

He shook his head and the cutest smile eked onto his face, but he didn't look at me. "My job now is to make sure you know how amazing I think you are. There's no humility in that. Let the world keep you humble."

I squeezed his hand tighter as we walked into his house, which brought Maribel and Ava's conversation in the kitchen to a hard stop.

Their friend Gabe was in the fridge, pulling out piles of raw meat, and he popped his head out to see what was going on.

I loosened my fingers under their scrutiny but Riah held tight. Right. We should just get this over with.

After a beat, Ava burst out laughing. Maribel looked to her, then back to us, only to mutter at her homework, "It's about time."

"Okay, but did he actually tell you he was crazy about you?" Gabe asked me. "Or did you have to bring it up first?"

Riah let go of my hand, but only to wrap his arm around me. "It was a joint effort."

Gabe laughed. "Sure it was." He stuck his head back in the fridge. "You hungry?"

Riah was always hungry. Wolves were always hungry. And just like that, everything felt normal again. Riah and Gabe shoving meat into their mouths, Maribel doing homework, Ava painting her nails. Riah and I had spent a lot of afternoons like this, with them, while Ethan and Stella took to her house. The four of us didn't frequent Ethan's basement the same as we used to, not after Samuel had been dismembered on Ethan's front lawn.

It seemed normal, but also like everything had changed. Every time Riah caught my eye, it felt like we were the only two in the room. And then he'd grin and I'd grin and—

"Gross," Maribel muttered, textbook still open.

Ava kicked my shin gently to get my attention. "What do you think?"

She was holding her hands out to me, her fingernails a sage green. "That's... my favorite color."

"Favorite color is a nice way to put it." Glancing up at me,

Maribel wrapped a finger around her braid. She had the darkest hair of the three of them, a deep chestnut. "It was a test."

Ava elbowed her.

"What are you testing?" I asked.

"How people give feedback."

I took a seat across from them at the small island. "And how'd I do?"

"Perfect, as usual." Ava rolled her eyes. "You managed to be truthful while also kind. Gabe, on the other hand..."

"Gabe said they made him want to vomit," Maribel cut in.

"And you?"

Maribel snorted. "I was with her when she bought it, when she said it was the color of something you'd pull out of your nose."

Riah washed his hands and came to sit next to me, his knee brushing up against mine in the process. My first reaction was to move away, even though when we were friends, it wouldn't have fazed me. I think he felt me twitch, because he slipped his hand on my knee to hold it there.

It hit me then, that there was no going back. Not that I wanted to, just that it was a whole lot heavier than anything had ever been with Christian. Because we couldn't break up and be friends again. And we couldn't break up and walk away, not as close as we already were. This was it. Monumental change. Pray God it would work.

I looked up from his hand to his face and he blushed, like he wasn't sure it was okay even though he could smell me. Even though I'd just kissed him like I was sure. So I slid a hand over his on my knee. He linked our fingers together and I had a sudden urge to rest my face in his neck.

Ava painted Gabe's nails and Maribel finished her homework with a lot of huffing and eye-rolling, not only about Riah and I, but also how distracting we all were. Still, she didn't go up to her room. And Riah and I leaned closer and closer into each other until I was nearly falling in his lap and he was pretty much holding me up.

"I should bring you home," he said at six o'clock.

I had to be home for dinner. He knew my schedule as well as he knew his own. How had I never realized what we were to each other before this? "I can bring myself home," I told him. My car was there.

He shook his head. "I'm not ready to leave you yet. Can I say that now?"

Ava gagged and Maribel threw her head down on her arms like she'd had enough. Gabe snickered.

I'm never ready to leave you, I replied.

"I see how it is." Riah grabbed my keys and stood. "Saying things in my head so everyone just thinks I'm a fool."

"You are a fool," Maribel agreed.

"Grace is the only not foolish thing you've ever done," Ava added.

And then we were out the front door into the waning sun-shine.

"You should stay for dinner," I told him. "Justin and Clara will be there." Justin and Clara were often there, at least for food. Well, food for my brother, anyway, being that Clara was a vampire.

He didn't reply, but when we were halfway to my house, he shifted in his seat to face me. "I've been holding this close for so long, it feels like my chest is cracked open. I think I need to get used to that feeling before Justin teases us in front of your dad."

That was fair. My brother could be relentless. "Okay. I get that."

Parking on the street since my brother's car was in the driveway, I got out and met Riah on the sidewalk. Resting a hand on his chest, I said, "I feel the same way. Like my chest is cracked open."

His hands skirted my waist as I reached my lips for his. Our kiss was slow, heavy with intent. But also short, because I was well aware someone might be watching—my parents, mainly. When he let me go, Riah took a few steps backward on the sidewalk and I headed for the house. Closing the door behind me, I pressed my back up against it, trying to collect myself before walking into the kitchen.

Justin appeared in the archway with a raised eyebrow. "What the hell was that?"

My heart reacted, beating harder as if I was in trouble, which was stupid. I wasn't in trouble. "What was what?" I asked, sweeping past him innocently.

"You and Riah. You're a *thing*?"

If he'd seen us kissing, there was no point in answering. I plucked a banana from the bowl on the counter instead.

Clara slapped it out of my hand. "Don't ruin your dinner."

"Not fair," I told her, noticing my parents at the kitchen table, staring at me. "You don't even eat dinner."

"It's true then?" my mom asked. "You and Riah?"

"How did I miss you all staring out the window?"

"Just me," my brother said. "But don't worry. I gave them a play-by-play."

I made a face at him and sat down at the table, sneaking a peek at the book my mom was reading. Trying to act like nothing had changed wasn't really working for me, but if I didn't, the flutter in my chest might take over.

"I'm not sure what to do about this," my dad muttered. "I can't stare down *Riah*."

He liked to intimidate my boyfriends. Christian handled it well, and Jeremy had been nervous every time, but Riah and my dad did dishes together. He'd been a staple at our house for about three years.

My mom went back to her book. "As if you didn't see it coming."

"I figured at this point, though, he'd never have the balls to do anything about it."

My brother snorted. "I figured, at this point, Grace would never have the balls to be honest about how she felt."

His words shook through me, because maybe this was what my dad was struggling with too. Maybe, for him, it wasn't about being honest with us, but being honest with himself.

If I'd left my family behind without a second glance, it would eat me up inside too. Maybe he had to tell himself he was an only child, in order to not be tortured by the truth.

Chapter Six

Exclusively Schmoozed

The November full moon, the first one since Riah and I became *Riah and I* drove all my reservations away for good.

It had always been hard, knowing he could get hurt—Aster had lost a twin to the hunt, and both Aster and Riah had a few nasty scars—but that night, locked up in my house so the wolves could prowl the town on four legs, knowing Riah was far away and hunting reasonably vicious animals? Let's just say I was beyond antsy by the time he walked into the lunchroom the next day. It didn't feel one bit awkward to wrap my arms around his neck, not even with the entire school there to see it.

He held me tight and we stood there until Aster groaned. "You were apart for less than twenty-four hours," she muttered.

I dropped my fingertips to his waist. Normally, I'd lift his shirt and inspect him for injuries, but doing that now—what I'd done a million times before—would feel all kinds of different. Stepping back instead, I cleared my throat.

Christian was frozen as we sat down, staring hard at the spot where I'd just been pressed up against Riah.

Jeremy, who'd been frowning at how Nathan's arm was tossed like an afterthought around Aster, glanced at him. "Wanna go play some ball till the bell rings?"

"Yes," he replied, decidedly, and they stood up as one.

Stella caught my eye. We'd already had a few discussions about how, since Nathan had shown up, Jeremy had been doing a lot of frowning. And how, since Jeremy, Christian, and Aster had started hanging out more, Jeremy had stopped dating. Which was a strange thing indeed.

As they disappeared into the gym, the principal and vice principal swept into the room and approached the two wolves closest to that hallway. They had short conversations with Nehemiah and Kiara, who gathered their things and followed them out.

"That's weird," I muttered.

"Weird that Nehemiah was called to the office?" Ethan asked, an eyebrow raised. But come on. How many times did I have to say it? He was not "trouble" just because he liked to leave town. Although, I guess he had beaten the crap out of Reilly last year. It was a long story that involved Reilly sneaking out of town to drink fresh and then letting Nehemiah take the blame for it. In a normal community. Where Nehemiah couldn't explain he was a wolf, and that a vampire was clearly the culprit. So, some might say Reilly deserved it.

Nathan snuck a pinky over for my pretzels and pulled the bag toward him.

"Does your dad not grocery shop?" I asked.

"Not really. He's kind of a mad scientist. Too preoccupied with his work."

"He's a *school teacher*."

"Dedicated to his subject. And his students. Speaking of, he's having a gathering after school if you all want to come."

"A gathering?" I raised an eyebrow.

"Yeah. He likes to get the kids together and promote unity or something." And with a wink, he peeled my banana like it was his own.

⟋⟍⟋⟍

Nathan and I walked to English together, as we did, now that he was my cousin. Insert eye roll.

"Aster say anything about our date?" he asked.

"What Aster tells her best friend is confidential."

"I'm going to assume it was all good then, if you're rooting against us."

I leveled a look at him as we sat down in class.

Nora dumped her backpack next to my chair. "I submitted my application last night."

I smiled at her. I knew. She'd messaged me, because I was the only other person, besides Riah, applying to UW Madison. She also announced it on her story. And made a post.

"I'm so nervous. What if I can't do it?"

"You can," I told her. "I promise." She was worried about living normal. Of course she was. Shady taught them it was nearly impossible.

"You're not going to change your mind, right? I can't do this alone."

"I'm not going to change my mind."

"What about Riah?" she asked, but before I could answer, Ms. Zieir started our discussion of Catch 22, and how the moral of the story could be applied to our lives and the existence of Shady Woods. Halfway through, our principal knocked on the door and called Gabe out of class.

Nehemiah, Kiara, and Gabe. All werewolves. What was going on that they were pulling werewolves?

I met up with Riah outside psych. "You talk to Kiara at all?" Kiara was his ex, and he had class with her after lunch.

"They asked her about last night. Seems like they're pulling everyone who hunted in Shady. But, as a wolf..." He trailed off.

I nodded. As a wolf, they wouldn't remember much but teeth and claws and meat and instinct. "Did someone die or something?"

He shrugged. "No one can figure it out."

⎯⎯ℓℓℓ⎯⎯

When Aster breezed in late to siren skills, she announced, "It's

Jess Hansen. Everyone's been talking, and Jess Hansen is missing."

Jess was a dendrite. A smart, cautious dendrite who never would have been out on the streets during a full moon. "That doesn't make sense."

"She's Emily's neighbor, and Emily said the cops were at her house this morning. She's for sure missing. Whether it has anything to do with the full moon, I don't know."

"If it had anything to do with the full moon," I pointed out, "they'd have a body." No wolf was in their right mind to clean up after themselves or hide a body, even if it was mostly just bones by the time they were done with it.

Aster checked the whiteboard, assessed the ingredients on our table, and leaned over the mixture I'd just slid past Nathan while eyeing the timer for when to put the next item in. We were to make a cleaning solution that would repel dirt for four to six weeks. Each of us had been assigned a window pane we were to clean with our result, and we'd be graded on efficacy in, you guessed it, four to six weeks.

"Do you think it could be Samuel?" I asked.

Aster frowned as she slipped the fish skin into the beaker. "Why would Samuel kidnap a dendrite during the full moon? That goes against his vision."

I chewed on my lip. That was true. He'd wanted to use Shady to show that everyone could get along—the wild abnormals and the domestic, so to speak. He'd been aiming for Shady to prove that the world could handle us being out in the open, while he worked on growing enough support with influencers in Holly-wood that the Elder Board and the Alpha Court couldn't shut him down.

That's when I remembered Elbie was in this class, in the back corner. Elbie was one of the wilds who'd come to town with Ethan's mom, and Ethan's mom was closer to Samuel than any-one else. So close that if we asked her whether she'd heard from him, she'd only tell us what Samuel wanted her to tell us. Elbie's loyalties weren't as strong.

Stalking over to him, I set a hip against his table.

"Grace." He nodded at me when I didn't speak right away. He was amiable like that, for a wild.

"Elbie." I nodded back to keep up with the niceties. "Have you heard from Samuel?"

"From what I hear, Samuel is in no state to contact anyone."

"And what is it you hear?"

"Don't you know someone on the Alpha Court?" The Alpha Court had been the ones to dismember Samuel last year—not necessarily a death sentence for a vampire—in order to keep the fact of our abnormal existence hidden.

I glanced at Aster. She was the one who knew someone on the Alpha Court, but he wasn't really allowed to communicate with his family anymore. "Please, Elbie? Tell me what you know. There's a girl missing."

"And you think Samuel's behind it?"

I nodded.

He shook his head. "No."

"Why not? How long does it take a vampire to recover from dismemberment?"

He snorted. "Who's ever been dismembered before?"

"You don't think, even a little bit, that Samuel could be behind this?"

"No, Grace, I don't."

"Why not?"

He rolled his eyes to me. "Aside from the fact that when they put him back together and left him bitten in the wilderness under a full moon, they figured he wouldn't make it through a second species transition?"

"Yes. Aside from that."

"If he did make it out, I guarantee he's in no position to stand, let alone steal a girl away or make any other big plans."

I stared at him as he grated the lemon peel, the ingredient not in the book that was key to a successful siren tear formula.

With a huff, he looked back over at me. "Is Violet still in town?"

I nodded. Ethan's mom shared Ethan's little sister's room. She'd taken to knitting and selling socks and sweaters at the boutique in town.

"When Samuel is with it enough, he'll call for her, and she'll go. Okay?"

I nodded. "Okay."

"Now shoo. You're distracting me."

But as I walked away, I wondered if it could be him behind it. No doubt he missed hunting. And he'd drained that body last year, to get suspicion off Nehemiah. He'd probably drained plenty in his lifetime. What was a little dendrite to him?

"Not Samuel," I muttered, as I returned to my friends.

"You know who's connected to Jess?" Jeremy asked. "Nathan."

My cousin threw his hands up in the air and turned to him. "Dude."

"Dude what? I saw you schmoozing her after school the other day."

Aster frowned. "I thought I was being exclusively schmoozed."

"I don't know what he's talking about," Nathan assured.

"Guess you'll have to prove it," Aster cooed, sidling up next to him. "After school."

"Vomit," Jeremy muttered.

"Don't you have your dad's thing?" I asked Nathan. And to Jeremy, *Did you really just accuse my cousin of disappearing a girl? I mean, I get he's super annoying, but...*

"You think I'm lying? I saw them together."

I turned around to study Jeremy. As long as I'd known him, he hadn't really been a liar. That being said, though, *I think you're jealous.*

He scoffed. And huffed. And flapped his lips.

Hey, Stella? She was in the next room, and I pulled Jeremy, Christian, Riah, and Ethan in on the conversation too. *I think it's time to start a list for Jeremy. Put Aster on it. And then Aster, and Aster, and only Aster.*

Christian snickered and Jeremy gaped at me. "Grace, I don't know what you're talking about."

"No? You don't?" With a grin, I turned back around. *Riah,*

does Jeremy smell like he has a thing for Aster?

"For longer than you smelled like you had a thing for me, if I'm being honest."

Chapter Seven

All Sorts of Weird

I hurried home from school because I knew it was one of the few afternoons I'd have the house to myself.

After having repeatedly hinted for more information to verify Nathan's story about our dads' childhood, along with a few outright asks, and after looking through every old photo album, not to mention all our storage boxes, it was time to search my parents' room.

I'll admit, it was a new low. I tried to tell myself that they'd read my diary if they thought I was keeping important secrets from them, but I'm not sure they would. Plus, I didn't keep a diary.

I started in my dad's small closet. Every suit coat pocket, every shoe box, every inch of the shelf. Then his dresser, even his underwear drawer, and between the summer clothes packed in flat containers under the bed. As I sat down next to his nightstand, I wondered what I was looking for, truly.

Proof that he cared about a sister he'd lost long ago? But I—my name—was proof.

Some sort of explanation for what was so horrible about her death that he could never talk about it? But a young girl dying was horrible, period.

Reasoning why he'd let us believe he was an only child all these years? That one I couldn't quite wrap my head around.

Opening the drawer in my dad's nightstand, the first thing I noticed was a bible. We'd gone to church on Christmas and Easter back in Chicago, but there were no churches in Shady Woods. Abnormals had faith in things one might associate with a higher power—like the force of nature and the world's intricacies being knit together by something larger than life—but religion was a human construct. I guess if you felt powerful and mighty, you didn't, as a rule, look to someone more powerful to guide you.

And before my brain went down the rabbit hole of whether or not we, as abnormals, worshiped our own strength—if that took our eyes away from a connectedness that would point to God—I pulled the bible out and set it on my lap.

It seemed strange that he'd have one. And that if he did, it wouldn't be tucked away somewhere. You only kept things in your nightstand that you wanted easy access to at night, when you were half asleep or unable to sleep at all.

Flipping through, I found three pictures I'd never seen before. One was tucked into the early pages of Genesis, of a woman crouched down next to a little boy. The back read "William, 1982."

Then, in the pages of Ruth, a picture of a whole family standing on the porch of an old farmhouse, no inscription on the back. I recognized my dad, probably about my age, my uncle, and a girl. The same woman who'd been in the first picture, and a severe-looking man with creases on his face that proved how much of his life he'd spent frowning.

The last was my dad and the girl, inside the book of Job. He was hugging her tight with one arm and they were laughing. The back said "William and Grace, 1995."

My fingertips traced her face and I realized it was her hair I'd inherited. I was taking a picture of the five of them with my phone when my mom appeared in the doorway.

Startled, I dropped the bible. As it fell off my lap, the photo drifted to the floor. My mom crossed her arms as I scrambled to put it back together. She stalked over to move the photo from where I'd stuffed it into a different spot, as if she knew exactly what page number he'd expect to find it tucked against.

Which led me to wonder what the page numbers meant.

I cleared my throat. "I thought you were meeting Riah's mom at the bookstore."

"And I thought you were going to your uncle's thing," she countered, taking the bible from me and setting it carefully back where I'd found it.

I closed the drawer. "How do you know about his thing?"

"He told us." My mom walked out of the room as if we weren't going to talk about what I found. "I figured you'd be there to help him feel more welcome," she added from the hall.

I followed her. "If he's doing this to feel more welcome, that's weird."

"He's always been a bit weird."

"I wouldn't know."

She turned on me at the bottom of the stairs, a harsh frown on her face. "I won't tell your dad you were snooping through his things."

"I wouldn't have to go through his things if he'd tell me a little something about my past."

"It's not your past, Grace. That's the thing. And it's very painful for him."

"Doesn't seem very painful when he's laughing with his brother and taking Nathan to lunch."

With a sigh, my mom disappeared into the kitchen. As I stepped through the archway, she opened the fridge and stared into it. "You've always been very good—maybe too good—living in the present. Can't you just do that now? Stop poking at a dead sister that only drudges up past horrors."

"So you admit it, that there was a sister."

"Go to the party, would you? Have fun. Be a teenager."

I opened my mouth to argue, but conveniently for her, Aster texted me: **i need you. pls come to your uncle's?**

⌇

My mom shouldn't have worried about my uncle feeling welcome. They'd been in town for maybe a month and it felt like half the school was at his house.

I wove through rooms stuffed with people but empty of things. Riah was at the town hall, copying documents that Ron wanted to get into the old council's hands, and before I could find Aster or Nathan, Nora grabbed my arm.

"I'm freaking out. I know you said I can do it, but Nathan told me seaweed isn't a regular item in a normal's diet. What am I going to eat?"

"You're going to eat seaweed. And raw fish. Just like you do now."

"But if people think that's not normal enough..."

"There's no normal enough. Normals are all over the place."

"He said normals only drink eight glasses of water a day—or less! That's not even half a gallon!"

"You're going to soak your feet every day and take long showers," I reminded, having already seen her map out how she was going to absorb enough water. "And no one needs to know how much water you drink."

"No one but you." She let go of me. "You really don't think anyone will notice?"

"Nora, they'll be so enamored with your poise and grace and beauty, they won't notice anything else."

She made a funny face. Here, in Shady, her poise and grace and beauty didn't stand out. All the sirens had poise and grace and beauty; the rest of us were used to it. Considering Nora was shy and a bit awkward, she hadn't been afforded the kind of adoration from the general public here that I knew she would there. Her shyness in Madison would come across as mysterious, her awkwardness cute. It was the way beauty translated in normal society.

"What if they don't put us together in the dorms, though. Then what?"

"They will. It's as simple as us both listing each other on the housing application, remember?"

She frowned. "You won't list Riah instead?"

"Why would I list Riah?"

Nora looked at me like I was stupid.

"Nora! We've only been dating a few weeks!"

"You've only been kissing a few weeks," she corrected. "You might as well have been married for the last three years."

I stammered, still not used to how unsurprised the school was over this recent development. "Well, okay, but no. Can I even do that?"

Her face drew a pinch of concern.

"I won't! I promise. I told you I'd room with you."

As a rule, I'd always been decidedly against ending up with a high school sweetheart. Yes, my parents had been high school sweethearts, and my brother and Clara, and my grandparents, but Charlie's parents met in college, and Mateo's had met at work after college. They all had stories and lives from before, stacked up like a building, where they'd done different, exciting things and experienced an array of worlds before settling down. That's what I'd always planned for myself.

If I couldn't imagine life without Riah, did that mean I was already settled down? That my life would end up a one-story ranch instead of a tall, dazzling tower?

I blinked at Nora. I couldn't talk about this anymore. "I have to find Aster."

"Last I saw her she was in the back hall."

Heading there, I found her with Nathan. They were a flurry of hands in the corner. Clearly her emergency wasn't so much an emergency anymore. I stood gaping at them for longer than I'd like to admit before pulling out my phone and texting Riah: **how come Aster and Nathan have known each other for five seconds and are more comfortable with each other than we are?**

i don't know what you mean, he replied. **i'm v comfortable with you.**

Then I realized what I'd done. I'd texted my best friend Riah my impulsive thoughts about how one of Nathan's hands was sneaking up under Aster's shirt in a crowded public space with his father in the next room, while I was flushed and embarrassed every time my hands wanted to simply slide up Riah's back. Over his shirt. In private.

But Riah wasn't just my best friend anymore. And I didn't exactly feel comfortable with him knowing that I wanted to slide my hands up his back. Preferably under his shirt.

Aster pulled away from Nathan to look at me. "Do you have to pee?" she asked.

"What?"

"You're fidgeting like you have to pee."

"Would I be standing here staring at you if I had to pee?"

"I don't know why you'd be standing here staring at me."

"You told me you needed me," I reminded.

"Oh, that." She nodded. "When I got here, Nathan was all over another girl."

"She was all over me," he corrected. "I can't help my animal magnetism."

Before I could even roll my eyes, Aster added, "I saved him. We're good." And they picked up right where they left off, full tongue exposure and everything.

I slipped through the nearest doorway to find myself in the kitchen, which was much less populated.

"Grace!" Kiara cried, like she was happy to see me, when she'd literally never been happy to see me before. Not when she and Riah were dating, and not anytime since.

I'd always found her a bit annoying. To be fair, that was because she'd always fawned over Riah, and I guess we knew now why that bothered me.

"With Jess missing, I had an idea about the wild wolves. I thought you could float it by Riah and see what he thought."

"You can ask him yourself, you know. You don't have to go through me."

She brushed her bangs back awkwardly. "I didn't want to step on your toes. And also, I couldn't find him. Are you in a fight? Is that why he isn't here?"

Okay, so maybe it wasn't entirely that she fawned over him that I didn't like. Maybe it was also because she was annoying.

"He's at work. He has a job."

"Oh, right. Well, want to hear my idea?"

My uncle was popping popcorn on the stove, chatting with the kid who was helping him. "Sure."

"It's called 'Take a Wild to the Wilderness.' I figured some of the wolf families who leave town for the full moon could bring a wild with them, like Riah's family did for me when I was first turned—I mean, it was so helpful. I couldn't have done it without him, not knowing anything about hunting—"

"The wilds know plenty about hunting, that's not the problem."

"But the whole point is showing them how we live, and that's how we're supposed to do it. Maybe it would help them with the transition, like it helped me with mine."

I stared at her. It wasn't a terrible idea, actually. "Riah might be able to get you a list of registered wilds from town hall," I offered.

Kiara smiled and squeezed my arm. "Great. I'll text him about it, if that's okay with you."

"Again, you don't have to go through me or ask my permission."

"I just don't want you thinking I'm trying to move in on him or anything."

"I don't." Or, I hadn't until she felt the need to say it.

"Oh! The movie's starting!"

I leaned against the doorframe between the kitchen and living room as she hustled off, and when the movie revealed itself as a rom-com, I decided to go pick up Riah from work.

———eee———

"Don't ask me to go back to that party," I told Riah, as he slid into my car.

"Yeah? Lots of crying about Jess and who might be next?"

"No. Not one mention of Jess." I'd sort of thought my uncle might decide it was an opportune time to organize us to look for her. Or collect any info we might have had about her whereabouts. "It was all snacks and making out. Actually, that's not true. Kiara has an idea."

"Yeah, she texted me."

I drove us toward the beach, in the opposite direction of either of our houses. "You hear anything about Jess at work?"

"Only that the town council thinks the Sentinel should head the investigation and the police chief lost his mind. They spent a lot of time in the conference room fighting about it, instead of actually doing anything."

I parked facing the water and told him about Aster's text, about how I rushed over there only to find her and Nathan making out in the hall, and about how Kiara assured me she wasn't trying to move in on him.

I'd always told him everything, but now I couldn't bring myself to go deeper. Couldn't peel back the layers of what had happened and tell him what I was thinking about it—that I wanted us to be Aster and Nathan at the end of the hall, or how at the same time, I was terrified of living a simple life. That I was worried he, and this town, would make for too simple of a life. Even so, I couldn't imagine leaving it. For college maybe, but not forever. And I was pretty sure leaving him would devastate me.

"So... the text you sent me about being comfortable..."—his brow furrowed—"That was about Aster and Nathan making out?"

I blinked. Shit. "Never mind. Forget it."

"Grace. I can smell you, remember?"

"I don't want to know what I smell like." For the first time ever, I did not want him to tell me what I smelled like. Particularly if what I smelled like was desire.

This was all so weird. Today was weird, full of contradictions at every turn, and yet I felt both sides so strongly. Wanting Aster to be happy but feeling like Nathan wasn't good for anybody. Wanting to know my cousin better, and my uncle, but being irritated with them for showing up and unearthing these secrets, which only made me doubt my dad. Wanting to jump in head-first with Riah but knowing it might not be what I ultimately wanted, which would just ruin the *us* that happened to be the most important thing to me.

Had I made a mistake letting our relationship get this far?

As if in response to this thought I hadn't shared, Riah drew me into a kiss that most definitely didn't feel like a mistake.

Why are you so much better at this than I am? I asked.

"At what?" he murmured, the vibration of his words on my lips.

At being comfortable with this. With us.

"I'm not doubting myself or my nose anymore."

I slowly pulled away from his kisses to study him.

"Not gonna lie, believing what I'm sensing off you is kind of intoxicating. Even if something is still a little off."

When I'd first moved here, he'd told me not to bother trying to hide anything from him. So, with a resigned sigh, I forced myself to explain. "I'm scared I'll never be able to walk away from you, and I'm not sure I want this life. I mean, I can't imagine walking away from Shady, but I always wanted something bigger, something wider. It almost makes me understand Samuel." Because if the world looked like he wanted it, I could have both. I could have it all. I stared at Riah in horror. "I can't believe I just said that."

He slipped his fingers through mine. "I'm going to college with you because I know all that. And I won't be what holds you back. College means maybe I can follow you wherever you go. Or maybe not. No pressure. Let's just see what happens, okay? And enjoy the ride?"

My heart collapsed a little at this, and it felt like relief, that he knew and understood me. Just like he always had.

And then I was kissing him, and he was kissing me, and I checked him over for full moon wounds like I'd wanted to in the lunchroom, only I kissed him while I did it, while I let my fingertips roam his back and sides and chest.

Beneath his shirt.

Chapter Eight

I Think You're Next

The dinner hour was in full swing and Parrino's was nuts.

I had the pizza pit, which was a handful of tables at the front of the restaurant on the bar side, up against the windows. The easiest section, if you asked me, aside from the fact that you had to weave through the bar crowd. Currently, my table of policemen was finishing up their pizza, and one of them was at the bar ordering another pitcher of beer. I'd been skirting around them all night, trying to think of an appropriate way to ask them about Jess's missing person investigation.

It should have made it easier that one of them was Ethan's uncle, who I ran into occasionally at his house, but that also meant he'd likely mention to Mr. Parrino that I stuck my nose where it didn't belong, and if there was one person in town who still intimidated me, it was Mr. Parrino.

One thing I noted was that it was definitely not a celebratory dinner. Not a work one, either, considering the number of pitchers I'd cleared from the table.

"This one is dying to ask us something," said the wolf, his nose twitching as I collected their plates.

I froze, my arm outstretched between Ethan's uncle and Officer Andres, who'd taken my statement last year when Mr. Turner had gotten murdered in the woods.

She looked up at me with a smile. "Go ahead and ask us, then."

I gathered the rest of their plates and swallowed hard.

"Don't be nervous," the wolf said. "We're no longer employed, so it doesn't much matter what we tell you."

"Archie, stop," Andres scolded. "We're not unemployed."

"We're also not exactly *employed*," Sergeant Parrino muttered.

I searched their expressions before changing my line of questioning. "What do you mean?"

"He means the town council is trying to disband us." Andres drained her glass, then pushed back and loped over to their fourth waiting at the bar.

The sergeant's eyes followed her as I tried to puzzle out what she was saying.

"They want the Sentinel to take our place," the wolf they'd called Archie explained.

My attention turned to him. "The Sentinel have no idea what they're doing. And I can say that. I have family on the Sentinel."

"Thank you for recognizing."

"Did this, like, *just* happen?" I asked, considering they were all still in uniform.

Ethan's uncle let out a heavy sigh. "Not exactly, but taking off the uniform feels like giving up. We're not ready to give up. "

"Particularly not on Jess," Archie added.

Oh! Perfect. "I heard the Sentinel were taking her case." My family on the Sentinel—Justin and Clara, who'd joined when its intent had been to protect the town—had confirmed what Riah overheard at town hall.

"They don't think her worthy of a case," Archie grumbled.

"And you do."

He studied me, forehead creased into a V above his nose. "Of course I do. There's no sign of her. And she didn't run away." He put a finger up at his sergeant, as if this was an argument they'd been having. "Not just because no one runs away from Shady, but because I've seen into enough of her life and I've been doing this a long time. The information *and* my gut are telling me she's here, somewhere, and she didn't disappear of her own accord. Plus, this stupid website? I don't buy it for a second."

"What website?"

Archie glanced at Sergeant Parrino, as if maybe he was looking for permission to keep going, but Parrino just waved his hand as the other two came back to the table. "We got an anonymous tip about a website that encourages people to put themselves in the path of a wolf."

"As if someone would be such a fan of a werewolf, they'd want to be chewed apart by one," Andres muttered.

"We were trying to source it, get some time data on it. But we no longer have access to anything."

"Does the Sentinel?" I asked.

"What?"

"Who has access now?"

Officer Parrino blinked at me.

"I have an idea." Collecting their napkins and silverware to pile on the stack of plates I was already balancing, I swung into the kitchen. Dumping it all on Jack, the dishwasher, I grabbed my phone out of my coat and texted my brother that I needed to talk to him later. Sergeant Parrino was at Ethan's on occasion, and my brother was at our house regularly. It seemed easy enough for us to shuffle information between the two. Plus, Ethan's house had access to the abandoned vampire tunnels beneath the town where the old council met secretly.

When I emerged from the kitchen with table two's pizza order, Aster, Christian, and Jeremy were at my empty table.

No Nathan? I asked Christian as I dropped the pies.

He had some last minute study thing, he replied, watching me as I made my way over.

I raised an eyebrow, because Nathan hadn't so far proven himself terribly studious, and it was a Saturday night. Christian shrugged, a smirk sliding onto his face as he inclined his head toward Jeremy, who was nudging Aster and whispering things in her direction. She seemed caught between a scowl and wanting to melt into him.

"Hello, my lovelies." I grinned. "A limeade, a cranberry juice, and a shot of rat's blood?" I knew well what my ex-boyfriend and best friend drank most regularly. The blood was a guess. It was what Jeremy had ordered on our first date.

He looked up at me with a little laugh. "Yeah, sure." When he melted his skin with fire, something he insisted impressed the opposite sex, the rat's blood healed him cleanly back up. "Hey, Aster, wanna see something cool?"

As I turned away, Christian caught my arm. "Can I talk to you when you go on break?"

I studied the siren shimmer in his ocean blue eyes. "Everything okay?"

He shook his head, but just barely. "When do you go on break?"

Riah walked up and slid a basket of bread onto their table, distracted at first by Jeremy's hand hovering over the candle. His attention then shot to where Christian held my arm. Chris must have noticed too, because he let go, and the feeling that settled in the pit of my stomach was surely a leftover from Christian's jealousy, from when I was dating him. Even though I knew Riah wasn't like that.

Right. Rat's blood. Before Jeremy's skin got so hot it dripped like wax onto the table. *Not sure I'll get a break,* I told Christian as I slipped away. *I'll find you if I have time.*

But then I realized Riah was here. And Riah filled in for many of us when we needed a break. I couldn't help it, I was curious. Christian didn't often seek out one-on-one conversations with me anymore. Maybe it was about Aster, something to do with

Jeremy and Nathan. Or maybe it was about... I couldn't think of anything else and then it got me worrying about Aster. Thanks to the cops staying to drink and another table ordering every dessert on the menu, I had a minute to find Riah. He was in the kitchen doing dishes, and I wrapped my arms around him from behind.

"I have two questions."

He twisted in my arms, careful not to get his soapy, wet hands on my white blouse or in my hair.

"One, are you okay?"

"Why wouldn't I be okay?"

I shrugged against him. "Christian."

"Touching you?"

I nodded.

"I can smell you, remember? And even if I couldn't, I'd like to believe I wouldn't be the jealous type."

I tilted my head at him and smiled, to which he caught my lips with his and drew me into a kiss as steamy as the sink behind him.

Jack came back from break and pretended to vomit in the wastebasket, which caught Robby's attention, who let out a loose whistle. I pulled away from Riah, hoping I wasn't blushing too bad, then said, *Okay, well, in that case, question two is if you'd cover for me so I could go on break and have a little private conversation with him.*

He raised an eyebrow. "Do you want me to be jealous?"

"No! No, I mean, he said he needed to talk to me."

His brow fell into a furrow.

"Mmhmm." I grinned. "So you're a little jealous."

"Not actually." He kissed me, short and quick. "It just reminds me of that entire year I *was* jealous."

"Please." I rolled my eyes. "The year I was dating him, you were dating Kiara."

"I tried really hard to like her." He kissed me on the nose. "But she was unfortunately not you."

I felt myself flush at that, at his words and the low, serious tone of his voice. Robby whistled again, a longer and lower note, and we weren't even kissing anymore, just staring at each other.

A soft smile broke out on Riah's face. "Go. See what he wants. You're losing time."

Right. Swinging out of the kitchen, I spotted Christian in the prep booth, trying to fold napkins and failing miserably. I plopped down opposite him.

"What are you doing over here?" I asked.

"Trying to give them some privacy."

We couldn't see the pizza pit because there was a wall that separated most of the bar from the dining room. "You think he has a chance?" I asked.

"She was in love with him in fifth and seventh grade, but don't tell her I told you that." He'd given up folding and was now just fiddling with a cloth napkin.

"I might absolutely love that for them."

"You're not on your cousin's side?"

"My cousin hasn't proven himself yet."

"Fair enough."

"Is that what this is about? Aster and Nathan and Jeremy?"

He shook his head, then rocked a little in the booth before spitting out, "I think you're next."

"What?"

"I think you're next. I've been having dreams again, and I don't think it's going to end with Jess."

He had portentous dreams, I'd give him that, but... "Maybe it's just that Jess isn't a one-off."

"Clearly, but it's also you."

I'd shown up in his dreams all last year. Because he hadn't been over me. And it didn't turn out the way he was worried it would. "Chris, I—"

"Stop, Grace, please. I'm not hung up on you anymore, I promise. Maribel and I have been talking. This isn't about that."

"Maribel?" As in Riah's sister? "You and Maribel?"

"Yeah."

"Chris, she's..." dark and mysterious and so not his type. Although, maybe that *was* his type; maybe I hadn't been. Sofia was dark and mysterious in a vicious way.

"You don't like her?" he asked.

"I love her."

"Good, then."

Good, then? Would this end up in some weird double date? I shook my head. "So you think Jess's disappearance is connected to me?"

"No. I think you're next."

"What do you see?"

"A room. A basement, really. And you. It's blurry."

"That's it?"

"That's it."

I stood up. Seeing as how, in my life here, I'd spent a considerable amount of time in Ethan's basement and currently had a plan to use it to connect my brother, the cops, and the council, I was going to attribute his dreams to that. Encouragement for a good idea, really.

"You're not worried?" he asked, following me as I headed back to my tables.

"I can take care of myself."

"You always say that," he grumbled.

"But now I mean it. I can aim an axe, and even without it, I can take down a vampire and a wolf. Riah and I still train, you know. A lot. In the woods."

He made a face.

"I'm serious. Heavy training. Multiple times a week."

"Yeah. Hot and heavy," he muttered, pushing past me.

With a frown, I called after him, "I thought you said you were over me."

As if on cue, Maribel popped through the door. Spotting me, she took the few steps from street level to the restaurant and gave me a quick hug.

"You and Chris..." I trailed off because over her shoulder, through the window, I saw Nathan on the sidewalk across the street. Walking with Cora. The girl he'd been "all over" at his uncle's party. Who he insisted had been "all over" him. The one he told Aster she'd saved him from.

"Yeah." Pulling back to look at me, she winced.

I waved her concern off and pointed to where he was sitting. As she squeezed my hand and left me, I shot a sharp, *What the hell, Nathan?* into my cousin's head. *Aster said you had a study group.*

If that's what she wants to believe of me, on a Saturday, then let her.

You didn't tell her that?

I didn't lie, if that's what you're asking. I said I had something to study.

Ugh. I hated him. I almost told Aster to look out the window right then, but she was laughing with Jeremy, leaning into him, and I figured that was better for her, to feel how it should be than to cry over what a complete and utter asshat my cousin was.

Maybe she'd choose Jeremy all on her own and I wouldn't have to be the one to break her heart.

Later, after punching out, I found Riah and Chris whispering by my car. Maribel was talking to Stella, who was waiting for Ethan to finish up inside.

Riah and Chris both looked in my direction, like my presence had interrupted something. I wandered over to see what was going on.

"Christian had a dream," Riah started.

Crossing my arms, I turned from my boyfriend to my ex. "We've been through this. And I know what it means. I just can't tell you, okay?"

"I told you she wouldn't take it seriously," Chris said to Riah.

"So you tattled on me to my boyfriend? He's not a body-guard."

"Maybe he should be."

"Oh, for the love. Where's Jeremy and Aster?"

"They went to a movie."

"Good. I hope a romance."

"Grace, I don't think you should brush this off."

"I'm brushing you off, Chris. Now go. You've set Riah on the job, so your work is done."

He glared at me and I glared at him, and then I snapped my fingers at Maribel. "I'm feeling done with him. Please take him away."

She wasn't one to be terribly obedient, but she loved me so didn't ask any questions. Slipping her arm in his, she guided him around the building to the street, where his car was likely parked.

"Is that not weird to you?" I asked, staring off at where they'd disappeared.

"Christian dreaming about you or him dating my sister?"

"The sister part."

"A little." Riah slid his hand through mine.

"I'm surprised she never mentioned it to me."

"You mean, like, got your permission?"

I stopped staring after them to catch his eye. "Of course not. She doesn't need my permission."

"Ava assured her you didn't like him anymore"—he tapped his nose to imply this was something Ava had verified by scent—"and that it would be more awkward to ask. I didn't want to speak for you. Or get involved, frankly."

Folding myself into him, I let my nose linger along his collarbone the way he'd taken to doing with me.

"But more importantly," he muttered against my hair, "you can't honestly think you're a better interpreter of Christian's dreams than he is."

With a sigh, I pulled away from him. "You, Ethan, and I need to talk. Then I need to catch my brother. Did you know the council booted the police out of their station?"

Chapter Nine

We're Not Official

On Sunday, I sent Aster a million texts about seeing Nathan with Cora the night before, only to delete each and every one. She was with him all day, and what if Cora hadn't meant anything? She'd been with Jeremy and would probably say that hadn't meant anything, so why did Nathan and Cora have to mean something?

By Monday, I'd nearly convinced myself of this and was leaning toward never telling her at all. But either way, I decided in first hour, if I *was* going to tell her, it wouldn't be in school. I'd found out about Christian between classes and that was terrible. I could at least wait until after school.

Then I caught Nathan winking at Cora as she walked by during lunch and I about lost my mind.

I threw my sandwich baggie at him. He pulled half of the sandwich out and slid the bag back to me.

"No." I threw it at him again. "What happened with you and Cora?"

The conversation around us came to a hard stop.

"Nothing," he grumbled between bites, eyes flitting to Cora's receding rear end.

I threw my orange at him. "You just winked at her when she walked by."

"I had something in my eye."

"Bullshit. You took her out on Saturday. I saw you."

"What are you talking about?" Aster asked. "Nathan, what's she talking about?"

"I saw Nathan and Cora on the street Saturday," I replied, at the same time my stupid cousin said, "Nothing."

"I was trying to figure out how to tell you," I mumbled, ashamed now that it had taken me so long, and doubly ashamed I hadn't been able to keep my stupid mouth shut until after school. Crying in the school bathroom was an experience I wouldn't wish on anybody.

With a sigh, as if my accusation had tired him, Nathan oriented himself more fully toward Aster. "Cora is disturbed, truly. She asked me to help her with calc and then some weird shit happened. I walked her home immediately."

"Bullshit," I said. "You don't live close enough to town to walk her home."

"We were at the library," he said, turning back enough to glance at me. "And let me tell you, it even made *me* uncomfortable, what she wanted to do in that library."

"Don't sex shame her to get yourself out of trouble," I snapped. "That doesn't mean she's disturbed."

"I've got this, Grace," Aster said, but it was like she was scolding me.

Riah leaned an arm around my chair and rubbed his nose along my temple, presumably to soothe me. Stella raised an eyebrow in my direction. Ethan and Christian were very intent on their blood and lunch, respectively, and Jeremy watched Aster carefully.

"What exactly happened in that library?" she asked.

"Not much." *Way to throw me under the bus,* Nathan muttered in my head. *We're family, remember?*

I don't give two shits about us being family. And you should *be under a bus.*

He only chuckled. *How'd that feel coming out of your mouth, such a big swear word?*

"Are you laughing at me?" Aster asked.

He straightened his expression. "No. I'm sorry. Grace said something—"

She snapped her fingers in his face. "Were you with Cora on Saturday?"

Nathan glanced at me, as if judging how it might go for him if he contradicted what I saw. Me. A dendrite who had a photographic memory and could send Aster a complete visual. A video reel, even.

With a scowl, he shrugged. "It's not like you and I are official."

Aster flapped her mouth open and closed a few times, then stood up, shoved her raw meat patty in his face and stormed off.

A chunk of ground beef fell from Nathan's chin to the table

with a plop. He wiped his face with my empty paper bag, then looked over at me. "I trust you'll pick up this mess you started." He motioned to her lunch. "I'm going to clean myself up and then do some damage control."

I checked on Aster, then fumed next to my cousin in English as we broke into groups to discuss the sirens in The Odyssey—what was accurate in their depiction versus what had contributed to current myths.

Nora started us off, and since Nathan and I weren't speaking, she kept going, laying it all out for us and then moving on to what sirens represented in Odysseus' journey—how they'd made him stronger and what he'd needed to learn from them.

Eventually, she gave up and asked, "Are you both coming to my New Year's Eve party?"

This did finally get us to look at her, rather than in opposite directions from each other.

"Rich is having a New Year's Eve party," Nathan said.

I rolled my eyes. "Of course he is."

"He's inviting the teachers too."

"Great. So you won't be at Nora's." I turned from him to smile at Nora. "Which means Aster and I will."

"You don't speak for Aster," Nathan muttered.

"Nor do you," I replied.

Nora grinned. "It's going to be great. Sofia and Elbie are even coming."

I raised an eyebrow. Sofia wasn't exactly nice to Nora. Or anyone. And since she'd started dating Elbie, she stopped caring about running the school, so I was surprised she'd go to any party, let alone Nora's. "You want her to?"

"I want everyone to. It's senior year, you know?" She narrowed her eyes at Nathan. "Though I suppose that might not happen if there are two parties."

He shrugged. "Sorry."

"Whatever," I said. "He just got here. Who cares about him?"

"Did I miss something?" Nora asked. "Aren't you two family?"

"Yes, Grace." Nathan cut me a look. "Aren't we family?"

"Aster was my family first," I replied.

"And Aster is my first choice," he countered.

"Then act like it," I snapped.

—eee—

In siren skills, Aster closed the space between us where Nathan normally stood and linked her arm through mine.

When Nathan walked up and realized we were squeezing him out, he slid in next to her, only for her to slowly move in that direction until he was standing back in the aisle.

Ms. Zieir raised an eyebrow at him as she cleared her throat. "Today we are preparing the formula for stain removal. This works on anything, hard surfaces and soft. You have thirty minutes to get it right and then we'll put it to the test. Please begin."

We were careful not to look in Nathan's direction, and eventually he took the hint, moving behind us to join Jeremy and Christian. But they'd been friends of Aster's way before I even showed up, and not only did they ignore him, but Jeremy also worked with flying elbows that kept jutting into Nathan as if he wasn't there.

He tried Riah and Ethan next, but the same thing happened there, so he settled at the corner of our table and dodged Aster as needed.

Christian started singing softly about "no longer putting up with his shit" as I mashed a banana until smooth and Aster dripped seven drops of siren tears from a dropper into a half cup of dish soap.

Jeremy joined in with Christian at the chorus, his voice hoarse and scratchy in comparison, and Aster frowned as she scooped some shortening out of its container and added it to the pulsating siren tear mixture, which crawled up the spoon to swallow every last bit of the shortening. I shuddered, remembering the time it crawled up my nose and into my lungs to help me breathe underwater.

When Nathan joined in at the second verse, Aster's head snapped up.

He sounded like my brother. Exactly like my brother. If I closed my eyes, I could imagine it was my brother when we were kids, singing in the car. Genetics were a funny thing.

"All right, kids." Ms. Zeier clapped once. "Now for the big test. Vampires, please cut yourselves. We need a strong ooze." Her heels clicked down the aisle as she peeked into our bowls. "Wipe that dark blood all over yourself and let's see who got this right."

I was looking at Nathan and Aster, realizing that none of us had that handy healing capability that was inherent in a vampire, when I felt arms wrap around me from behind.

"You're very welcome," Jeremy said, dragging the open cuts on his palms across my light blue shirt. He held his hands up and we watched as the slashes he'd made in them, thanks to the box cutters Ms. Zieir had provided, healed over before our very eyes.

"Amazing." I shook my head. "Gets me every time."

He went to wash his hands and Aster turned her back to Nathan in order to slather the siren solution on me. It tickled as it moved along the threads of cotton, so much so I had to hold my shirt out, away from my skin. After we'd added the shortening, it had turned a warm gold, but as it worked on the stain, it faded to clear and then disappeared into a smoky mist.

Voila. And I was clean.

"Siren tears," I muttered, shaking my head and running my hand along the fabric. It left nothing. No residue, no moisture, no stain. "Also gets me every time."

Christian started belting out the chorus of the song again, and Nathan looked like he might punch him.

"What about Constantine?" Nathan asked, his tone vicious. "I heard he likes to drag victims into the tunnels. Jess is probably down there and nobody has checked."

I had to hand it to him, it might have been an effective diversion, if it weren't for the fact that Constantine, the cellar's bloodtender at Parrino's, was as gentle as a cat. Which was about as gentle as you could ask a vampire to be.

"What do you know about Constantine?" I asked. Or the tunnels, I wanted to add. Because the old council met down there, so if there was a body, it would have been found. No one was supposed to know that though.

"I know he's bloodthirsty."

"We're all bloodthirsty," Jeremy muttered.

"She went missing on the full moon," Riah added. "No one's looking at a vampire. Even a vampire wouldn't have been fast enough to drag a body through the streets and not get mauled by a wolf."

"Besides," I said, "if I had to put money on a vampire, it would most definitely be Elbie."

In a vampire second, I felt hot breath on my ear. With a yelp, I turned to find Elbie himself, so close he'd nearly been wrapped around me. He tapped his ear, as if I'd forgotten vampires had insane hearing abilities. "I'd put money on that Reilly kid," he said.

"If I had to put money on someone, it would be you. Not Reilly."

"But I'm domesticated now."

"If Sofia is your standard of domestication, I promise you're only halfway there."

"I've turned from my ways, okay?"

"But have you turned from Samuel?"

Elbie laughed. "You're really obsessed with him, aren't you?

I'll let him know you've got a crush." And with that, he blew me a kiss and sped back to his lab partner.

Chapter Ten

Yuletide

We had longstanding holiday traditions with my mom's parents, because when we lived in Chicago, we'd always visit during Christmas break. That was when normals traveled for family, so it was when we traveled for family.

My uncle, however, thought this year would be a great time to create new traditions.

Christmas eve stayed the same. My mom wouldn't compromise on that. There was a little chapel out in the woods with no walls and only a few rows of pews. Grandma always led us there at midnight with lit candles, and we'd leave them in the snow for the people we'd lost.

Now I knew why my dad always brought three. One for his mom, one for his sister that I'd assumed had been for his dad, and one for his long-lost brother, based on the fact that this year, he brought only two.

Christmas dinner, though, my uncle was hosting. He'd even

talked my parents into sleeping over, so we could open presents under the tree in the morning, like he and my dad had supposedly done when they were little.

I wouldn't know of course, because my dad wouldn't talk about it. But I guess that was the bonus of actually getting to know my uncle. He might answer some questions.

I should've been glad for the distraction, this second full moon since Riah and I were official, but I was still pissed at Nathan about Cora. And my uncle had thrown my overnight bag on his top bunk.

While our parents rehashed their childhood, still completely omitting any mention of the sister I was named after, I told Nathan that I wasn't sleeping in his room.

Afraid you won't be able to control yourself? he asked.

It's clearly you who can't control yourself.

If this is about Cora, then I presume you're also mad at Aster for studying with Jeremy every chance she gets. Just the two of them. From what I've gathered, he doesn't study textbooks, if you know what I mean.

Which shut me up pretty quickly. Even so, he continued inserting similar thoughts into my brain throughout the rest of the meal, like, *if she commits to me, I'll commit to her.*

And what could I say to that? I'd been the one begging her not to take Nathan seriously. By the time we were sitting over dessert, he nearly had me feeling like it was all my fault—as if I'd pushed him to Cora by pushing Aster toward Jeremy.

My brother clapped his hands against the edge of the table,

pushing away from his untouched pie, and stood up. "We better get going if we want to make it home before civil twilight."

Civil, nautical, then astronomical. After that, the sky went black and the wolves woke to the full moon.

My uncle jumped up to grab their gifts from under the tree and walked Justin and Clara to the door. The rest of us finished our pie and cleared the table. When the kitchen was clean, our parents left Nathan and I to pore over my uncle's record collection in the living room.

Nathan rolled his eyes as they started arguing about what to listen to first, grabbed my hand, and led me up the stairs.

Besides the bunk bed, his room held a bean bag chair and a desk. Plopping onto the chair, he asked, "Apple or pumpkin?" referring to the pie we'd just eaten.

"Pecan," I replied. "Green bean or sweet potato casserole?"

"Sweet potato," he said. "Chest or butt?"

"What?"

"On a turkey or a human. Chest on both, for me."

I wrinkled my nose, but to be a good sport, replied, "Thigh on a chicken. Chest on a guy."

He smirked, then stood and went to his closet. When it was clear he was going to change into pajamas in front of me, I grabbed my bag and slipped out to find the bathroom.

By the time I was ready for bed—teeth flossed and brushed, face washed, and in my Christmas pjs that matched his, my uncle's, my parent's, and my brother's—he was already tucked in, almost as if his dad had stopped by and literally tucked his sheets in around him. I crawled up top and got comfortable.

"Siren or wolf?" he asked, once we'd both stopped rustling around.

"Wolf." And with this, I checked the full moon out the window, feeling a tug on my heart that Riah would be losing himself to it soon. "Dendrite or wolf?" I asked, because he'd said he had a thing for dendrites the first day I met him. But Aster was most certainly a wolf.

"Dendrite," he replied. "Living normal or living in Shady?"

I sighed. "Shady is too small, don't you think?"

"Yeah, I'd choose normal every time."

But the people here—living comfortably around abnormals—was something I knew I'd never be able to replicate in the normal world, even if I brough Riah with me. I peeked over the side of the bed. "Don't you feel more at home here, though? In a community that allows you to be yourself?"

"*A.* I've never lived anywhere long enough to feel like it was home. And *B.* I'm constantly worried dendrites are trying to control me. Which means *C.* The only peace I get is around normals, when I easily have the upper hand."

I rolled my eyes as I laid back. "Dendrites don't control minds."

"Don't they?"

"*Master it, hide it, keep it,*" I reminded. It was the dendrite mantra to ensure we did no harm.

"You're assuming everyone's honorable enough to follow that," he muttered.

"Have you met so many dishonorable people?"

"It only takes one."

A silence fell and a howl sounded in the distance. It would be easier to manipulate a normal, of course, since they didn't know such a thing as a dendrite even existed. My mom, well before I was able to speak in anyone's mind, always made sure I knew how big of a responsibility it was to do no harm, to not use our powers for manipulation. But I guess, if you weren't honorable, you could place thoughts and make a person feel things they didn't actually feel.

I was about to ask him who he'd met and what they'd done to him, but he started snoring. Eventually, I drifted off too, only to wake a few hours later due to a thump.

I shot up in bed, heart racing, thinking of how it sounded like the werewolf who'd hit the floor in our back hall after my dad sheared its head off.

It was the full moon now, just like then.

It took me a second to orient myself before I realized where I was. Nathan was stumbling out of the room and had probably ran into his desk. For a second, I thought he might be going to the bathroom, but he hit the doorframe hard on his way out into the hall. As if he was drunk or somewhat disoriented.

I hopped down from the bunk and found him sitting at the top of the stairs, his hands clutching his head, breath frantic.

"Nathan?" I whispered, setting fingertips on his shoulder.

With a yelp, he shot up and nearly knocked me over. Eyes wide with horror, he raced down the stairs.

"Nathan!" I hissed, hurrying after him.

Oblivious to my calls or my presence, he seemed to be searching for something, room by room on the main level of the house. Catching him by his shoulders as he spun to rush past me again, I shook him. "Nate!" It was what my parents called him. "Wake up!"

He snarled, maybe because he felt like I was holding him down, so I let go, only for him to throw a lazy left hook. I caught it in my fist, then ducked as he tried to swipe me out of the way with his other arm.

Being thwarted twice threw him into a fury, and his fists came at me like I was a punching bag. I dodged a few, took one that bounced off my side, and spun around him to hook my arms through the crooks of his elbows from behind.

Both of our bodies heaved with the unexpected exertion, and as I locked him to me, I hissed his name again in his ear. In his head too, *What in the* hell, Nate. Wake up!

His breathing slowed and his muscles relaxed, then he was sliding out of my grip onto the floor. Ethan had used this on me once when we were sparring—a ploy to make me think he was surrendering when really he wasn't—and before I could wrap my head around the fact that I was *sparring with a nightmare,* Nathan's shoulders began to shake. Staying out of his reach, I stepped around to face him.

Tears glistened on his cheeks in the moonlight and he looked through me, like I wasn't even there. In his crouch, he started shaking his head, muttering "I'm sorry" over and over again.

Still, though, I didn't think he was apologizing to me—his

expression was glazed, like he couldn't see me clearly. Or this room. Or this night.

Footsteps on the stairs revealed my uncle in a robe.

"Nathan." It was a harsher tone than I'd ever heard out of him.

At my uncle's voice, Nate shot up and ran to the back door. My uncle charged, catching him just as he went for the door handle, then slapped him across the face with a loud smack. I jumped at the sound and took a step back, my stomach tightening.

"Night terrors," my uncle explained. "On the full moon." He glanced at me. "Bad combo."

"Dad?" Nate's voice echoed, weak and high like a little boy.

"It's all right, son." Gathering him in his arms, he hugged him tight. Their silhouettes were outlined by the bright light of the moon streaming in the little panes of the door. "You're safe now. It's over."

Safe from what, though? What had he been sorry for?

My uncle nearly dragged Nate up the stairs and back to his bed, where he gently tucked him in. I stood in the middle of the room as he stepped around me and slid a key into my hand. "Lock him in," he muttered. "I don't want him to be the next one, lost to a wolf."

It was a few long minutes before I did though, and when I turned back around, Nate was watching me.

"Are you okay?" I asked.

"They're about my mom, the night terrors."

"What about her?"

"I found her. Head smashed in like a wolf..." He turned away from me, his back to the room.

Sitting down next to him, I considered loosening the sheets so he could sit up and I could hug him. But maybe that was weird. He might be family, but until tonight he hadn't felt like it.

His soft blond hair brushed against my elbow, and I felt his ache as it leached into me, as he shared the emotion, most likely without realizing it.

I sat there, connected but barely touching my cousin, who was broken and flayed open, until he fell asleep.

◆◆◆

I woke early, like I tended to do mornings after the full moon. Nate was sleeping like an angel and my phone was in the kitchen. I needed to check it. Riah and Aster always texted me to let me know they were safe.

Yes, it was ironic to worry about the big bad wolves being safe, rather than those they might come into contact with. But Riah hunted powerful things with bigger teeth and larger claws than he had, and accidents happened.

Aster had been hunting in town since her dad joined the Alpha Court, so I was less worried about her, but town wasn't what it used to be either.

Padding into the kitchen, I found my uncle at the table with a steaming cup of black coffee. Perfect. I could ask him all the questions before my parents woke up and stared at me with a look that implied it was none of my business and I was only going to piss them both off.

"Nate told me about Grace," I started, before I realized what a lousy good morning such a comment was. "I didn't even know there was a Grace. Before me, I mean. Guess I never knew there was a *you*, either."

My uncle looked up at me, his face drawn. "It wasn't suicide, if that's what you're worried about."

"That..." wasn't what I'd been worried about. But, if it wasn't suicide... "She died of natural causes?"

He shook his head and slid the newspaper over to me. "Look."

But I didn't care about the newspaper. If it wasn't from natural causes, and it wasn't suicide, then that didn't leave much but murder. My aunt had been murdered? It took me a minute to choke out, "Who killed her?"

"We don't know if she's dead yet. She just went missing last night."

"What?"

"Sasha." He nodded to the newspaper and pinched his nose. "Nathan was so close to walking outside." Then he was up, shuffling out of the room, mumbling about how to lock the doors from the outside, to keep him safe.

I plunked hard into the chair he'd left, my fingertips drifting to the article. I should read it. Worry should be consuming me. Christian had said I was next.

Though, clearly I hadn't been.

What *was* consuming me was my aunt's possibly unsolved murder. Unsolved, because, according to my cousin, our grandpa covered it up to protect his sons. To protect Shady's secret.

No wonder he blamed them.

And no wonder my dad couldn't talk about it.

Chapter Eleven

Snatching Feed

People were saying that two girls were lost to the wild.

As if missing teenagers were a natural hiccup in the world of abnormals, an occurrence to be expected when one lived among beasts, even though that had never been the case before. Not when Shady was formed, and not when my parents were growing up.

This was a new generation, they said, formed with the kind of kids who might throw themselves in front of a wolf on purpose. At least, if this "Something Paranormal" online forum the cops had been talking about was to be believed.

I mean, I guess I did believe it. I was of the generation they were talking about, and I'd seen weirder things than that online. If you were feeling particularly helpless and weak, and you believed becoming a werewolf could fix that for you, then sure, it might seem like a good option. But Jess and Sasha knew a wolf on the full moon would do nothing more than attack.

All I could do was hold onto the fact that my brother, Ethan's uncle, and the old town council were working together. They'd figure it out. They'd find them. They had to.

Until then, life went on. Even and including Nora's New Year's Eve party.

Her house was distracting, so there was that. Since it was really a front for their home underwater in Iara, they didn't use the space the way most would. For example, there was a pool table in the dining room, a putting green in the kitchen, and random human things packed into the two bedrooms: an old school desk, the kind where you lift up the top and store your things inside, a spinning wheel halfway through creating a ball of yarn, and a tea set laid out properly on a bistro table. Like they were collectors. A pair of skis were propped up next to a pair of crutches and a surfboard, and a collection of feather boas and old hats rested on and around mannequin heads, which sat above slippers that seemed to have never been worn. The list went on, everything lined up layer after layer, with only a few pockets here and there to get around in.

The living room was the only accurately represented room in the house, aside from the floor lamps dressed with long women's skirts and the fact that the pictures on the walls were hung upside down.

Nora found me in the living room, where I was studying one of these pictures. She offered me a cup of giggle juice. "Fresh batch," she said. "It's delish."

I took it from her and she made an excited but terrified face.

"To UW!"

Clinking glasses, we drank. Our emails had come, along with Aster and Christian's acceptance letters for Minnesota, but Riah had been deferred. He'd been standing with me, hand on my back, and at Nora's toast, I felt it drop.

"Oh!" Nora said to him. "I'll get you one too."

"Don't bother. I'm not celebrating." He caught the concerned look I gave him and added, "I mean, I'm celebrating you two, of course."

"You'll get in," I assured, though I couldn't know that. "Or we'll go to Minnesota."

"Grace, no!" Nora cried, shaking her hand in front of her chest as if she might have a panic attack at the thought of going to UW without me.

My stupid big mouth. And when I could've used my brain, too. "Just kidding," I told her. "Riah can go to Madison College."

He raised an eyebrow at me, as if I was now picking Nora over him, and I considered fogging them both to start over. My mom would kill me, though, and Nate's comments about mind control had me wondering lately what little ways I might be manipulating people without really thinking about it. Fogging would definitely be one of them.

I handed Nora the rest of my giggle juice and encouraged her to drink it—not that it relaxed you exactly. It should make things feel lighter though. A shout came from the kitchen and she nodded, tossed the rest of my glass back, and spun on her heel.

Riah's expression was dark. Maybe as unhappy as I'd ever seen it. He slumped down on the couch and I joined him, landing so close that I could see the soft dusting of freckles across his nose.

"You'll get in," I told him.

"Maybe I'm not supposed to."

"What are you talking about?"

"Maybe I should be as worried about living normal as Nora is. Or maybe I should be more concerned that it's me who will hold you back, not Shady."

"Riah—"

He shook his head, then let it drop back on the couch and closed his eyes.

I opened my mouth to say something else, not that I knew what that might be, when I caught sight of Sofia charging toward me.

Hands on her hips, her stick-straight hair sweeping low past her stick-straight vampire torso, she stopped to loom over where I sat. "You accused my boyfriend of snatching feed?"

Riah opened one eye and I set my jaw. I would not have a conversation with her if she referred to my kind as feed, or sheep, or anything that made up a herd.

"You leave him alone this instant. Do you hear me?"

I let out a short laugh. "Was he intimidated?"

Elbie appeared behind her and answered for himself, "No, he was not." Then he looked at her. "What are you doing?"

"I'm reminding her what's mine, as she has so often liked to take it."

I snorted. "Really? You think I'd go for Elbie? Or that he'd even have me after I hurt his wittle feelings?"

"I don't have feelings," he snapped. But his expression, as it softened on Sofia, told me something else. "Come on. Let's go."

Sofia hadn't taken her eyes off me. "He's not involved, do you understand?"

"Does that mean you know who is?" Riah asked, now fully invested in the conversation.

"No," she snapped. "It means I know how Grace likes to stick her head in things. And I want to remind everyone that Elbie only did what he did last year to save one of us—an innocent Shady citizen he didn't give two craps about." Her glare swung to Riah for a second, then back to me. "So you better not use that against him when you go on whatever crusade you have planned. Leave him out of it and leave us alone. Got it?"

We stared at each other for a beat and I nodded. I could give her that, I supposed, if she felt so passionately about it. At least for the time being.

Elbie slid his spaghetti noodle arms around her waist and pulled her back through the crowd. She made sure to walk around Aster and Jeremy, which was incredible. Not just because Aster and Jeremy were making out like it was New Year's Eve and tomorrow was the apocalypse, but because Sofia didn't walk around anyone. Generally, she made her own path, and if you happened to be in it and didn't move of your own accord, then watch out.

Before I could elbow Riah and point out Aster and Jeremy, the crowd parted like the Red Sea. Through it flowed bulky Sentinel in fresh new gear, streaming from the front door to infest the party.

"What are they doing here?" Riah asked. Because they'd been formed to keep the unsavory out of Shady Woods. Which had nothing to do with a high school party.

Unless they'd found one of the girls.

Grace, where are you? my brother asked in my head.

Living room. What's going on?

Looking for Cora.

My skin pickled. *Cora?*

His head bobbed above the crowd, Clara's dark hair doing the same behind him. *Her parents called her in missing. We're checking all the parties she was invited to tonight to make sure it's not a misunderstanding.*

I haven't seen her.

He found me, setting his hands on his hips. His expression was as unsettled as I'd ever seen him. *You're okay?* he asked.

As unsettled as I could ever imagine him being. *Have you been to the other party?*

Yeah, and Nate said she was here.

I swallowed this news, tasted and digested it. It didn't go down so well. My cousin had been seen with her, enough to clearly have some sort of relationship with her. Now she was missing and he supposedly knew her whereabouts?

"I haven't seen her all night," I assured, scanning through the pictures in my head that cemented themselves more firmly than other species' memories, checking every face. "She's never been here." Which meant, if she'd gone to a party, it had to have been the other one.

I have a thing for dendrites, he'd said.

"Maybe it's Nathan," I muttered to Riah. "Could it be Nathan?" I asked my brother.

Except, Nathan had an alibi for girl #2. Me. I was his alibi the night Sasha went missing.

Before I could ask Justin what three girls meant—and one disappearing not on a full moon—four sets of headlights swung across the front windows.

Police cruisers. Straight up on the lawn. Their lights flashing red and blue, reaching into the dark room and slashing across our faces.

The Sentinel collectively stiffened, and the one in the middle of the pack motioned for a few to check the kitchen and bedrooms, then led the rest out the front door to stand sentry on the porch.

I glanced at my brother, who was frowning so deep he was earning lines on his forehead that resembled our dad's.

"Council says it's a wild issue," Justin muttered. "Our jurisdiction. Obviously the cops don't agree."

"Council's awake right now?" I replied bitterly. "Working?"

"Well,"—my brother nodded to the burly guy on the front porch who was stepping down to talk to Officer Parrino—"Adam's on the council. And he said."

"He can't do that, can he?" Riah asked. "He can't be both."

Justin's jaw twitched as he watched whatever part of the interaction happening out front he could see from where he stood.

Clara glanced at him, distracted, then to me. "Cora slept at a friend's house last night, but the friend woke up to her missing this morning. No one's been able to get ahold of her all day. Checking the parties was a last resort."

I glanced at Aster, who'd been with Nate the night before, but before I could call her over to ask how long she could vouch for him, Sofia charged toward me.

No words this time, no sparring, just spiked nails piercing my cheek and dragging their way through my skin.

Dang, that stung.

All those hours of training kicked in, and without thinking, I tripped her off balance, grabbed her arm as she fell, and spun her so she landed face down on the floor. With one foot on her back to hold her there, I twisted her arm in my hands, putting pressure on her shoulder joint.

"What the hell was that for?" I asked, the slices in my cheeks burning.

A commotion caught my eye as two Sentinel dragged Elbie into the living room, his hands cuffed behind his back.

Oh.

Sofia's body went slack and she let out a whimper as they swept him through the front door.

I let her go, and in an instant, I was on the ground. On top of me, her hair hanging around my face like a curtain, she bared her fangs. "I will end you."

I slammed my forehead against her face, and as she let go of me to cover her oozing nostrils, I flipped us over. Sofia was scrappy but had no skill, and with little effort, I was on my feet, her wrist twisted in my hand and my shoe on her hair to hold her down.

"This wasn't me," I told her.

"They said he has three classes with her. That he's the only wild in her classes. And someone told them he drank that body last year." She speared me with a look. "He did that to save Nehemiah! Because I asked him to. He was protecting an innocent Shady citizen!"

Tears filled her eyes and this unsettled me more than most things might. Against my better judgment, I moved my foot from holding her hair down and let her go.

"It wasn't me, Sofia. I promise."

Nursing her wrist with her other hand, she stood up and looked to my brother and Clara. "He was with me all last night. But they won't listen."

"The police will," I told her, and all of us were drawn to the light scuffle that was happening outside—the police trying to muscle their way in as the Sentinel tried to muscle their way out.

"The police don't matter anymore," Clara said, her words clipped, because it was what she was supposed to say. "But we'll do what we can." With a nod for Sofia, she led my brother through the living room to follow their Sentinel back to whatever hole they'd crawled out of.

Sofia moved to watch from the window, and Nora slid in front of me, a red solo cup filled with a shallow pool of fresh siren tears in her hand.

I nodded. Usually Stella healed me, but I hadn't seen her since she and Ethan went for a walk on the frozen lake.

"One girl could be a fluke," she muttered as she worked her tears into the cuts Sofia had dug into my face and neck. "But two is no coincidence."

"What about three?" I winced as the siren tears wiggled in the wounds and stitched my skin back together. "Three is a pattern."

Riah crossed his arms, gaze set on the chaos still churning out on the front lawn. "And patterns repeat."

Chapter Twelve

Anyone Have Some Popcorn?

The high school had a way of absorbing clues and dumping them into our collective consciousness, and within a few days, we all knew the details surrounding Cora's disappearance.

Everything Justin had said was true, of course, but first hour in human history, Gabe showed us some messages from that stupid wolf forum where @coralane had set up to meet a wild at the truck stop. She didn't want to disappear, it said, but she did want to become one of them.

Supposedly. But that begged the question where she'd gone. She hadn't written about wanting to leave Shady or live wild. Just that she wanted to be stronger and more formidable.

Fair enough. It was why I trained with Riah.

In second hour, I asked Jeremy if anyone had actually been

at the truck stop New Year's Eve, or the night before. Alarms would have gone off at his house if anyone had shown up at the attached diner, drove through the parking lot, or even passed on the road in front of it, because Jeremy's dad was the original Shady keeper—the original Sentinel, so to speak, tasked to keep people out. The truck stop was open all night to encourage wayward strangers to stay on path, up or down the highway, rather than them getting curious about the little dirt road that snaked behind the gas pumps.

In case his dad wanted to go home, or to alert his family that he might need backup, any car that passed, even if they didn't stop, set off an alert at Jeremy's house. It wasn't common knowledge that their house was rigged up like this, but the fact that those alarms had been silent when Cora was supposed to meet someone there proved she never made it. And neither had her wolf.

Which meant what? The meetup was a smokescreen? Or she'd met him somewhere else?

I texted my brother, and I texted Ethan to text Sergeant Parrino.

In calc, my uncle leaned against the front of his desk and droned on about support and coming together and how he hoped to create a safe space for anyone who was troubled like those missing girls and might be planning a way out.

"Troubled?" I muttered, loud enough for the room to turn and look at me. "Who told you they were troubled?" Had Nate told him Cora was troubled?

"No one had to tell me, Grace. All teens are troubled." He

delivered this with a soft smile.

"I'm not," I said tightly, trying to control my frustration lest I seem *troubled*.

"No?" he countered. "You have no issues with any members of your family?"

I stared at him for a moment, struggling to decide if he was referring to something my dad might have told him about how I acted when I found out about his existence.

Turning back to the room as a whole, he continued, "It's always been hard, growing up. But now, with the temperature in town, the way everyone is split between living out loud and living like old Shady, it must be even more confusing."

I tried to shut him out the rest of class, and when I couldn't take it anymore, I grabbed the bathroom pass and left for the quiet of the hall.

At lunch, I plopped into my seat just in time to see Christian present Maribel with a poster at the next table over. He was wearing fake fangs, had slicked his hair back like Dracula, and was wearing nothing but jeans and a cape. The poster read "Be my vamp-entine?"

"That's early," I noted. There was a month and a half still until the Valentine's dance.

Aster had her chin on her hand and was smiling at them dreamily.

"Is it his chest you're smiling at, or the gesture?" Nate grumbled.

She winked at him. "It's okay for you to smile at his chest too.

It's a nice one."

"I'm confused why he had to take his shirt off though," Jeremy muttered, his eyes cutting to Aster's face.

I laughed.

"What?" he snapped.

"You're beautiful too, Jeremy, just in a different way."

"It is hard to measure up," Riah said, but without any bitterness. I rolled my eyes to him. His chest measured up just fine. He was, after all, a wolf. Wolves were positively corded with muscle. Christian was a dendrite trapped in a siren's body, which meant he might be breathtaking, but he wasn't ripped. Jeremy, being a vampire, had the most trouble bulking up, and my cousin was pretty wiry himself.

I handed one side of my peanut butter and jelly to Nate. "Neither of you want to take Maribel to the dance, so I'm not sure what you're jealous about."

Aster frowned and stood, then looked pointedly at me and Stella. *Come along,* was what her expression said. I grabbed my granola bar, shoving the rest of my lunch over to Nathan, and Stella gathered her bottles of water. Aster led us to the quiet corner at the end of the library's hall.

"Do you think dendrites can plant thoughts?" she asked, pacing the short width of it. I settled on the windowsill and Stella sat on the floor, her water lined up next to me.

I looked at her strangely. "You know we can place thoughts."

"Not just place. Something more than that. Do you think you could control a mind if you wanted to? Set things in motion and then let them go and watch them grow?" She stopped for a moment to glance at me. "Don't think I'm crazy."

"I don't think you're crazy. I'm just confused."

"When I come back from the full moon, I want Jeremy. I miss *Jeremy*. And it's so easy with him. It's like the full moon untethers me from this life and resets me, but then Nathan shows up and messes with my mind or something and I'm confused again."

Stella finished draining a bottle of water and set it on the floor. "Sounds like you're torn between two hot guys."

"Dendrites can't control minds, Aster." I delivered this as gently as possible. "We can't poke around in there."

"But you can make people forget, and you can bleed emotion into them, and drop thoughts they'll think are their own."

"Not long term."

"I know! That's my point!" She threw her hands up. "It lasts the month, the moon wears it off, and he starts over."

"A month is pretty long term, if you ask me."

"Forget it," she muttered. "You don't understand."

I raised an eyebrow. "I don't understand being torn between two guys?"

She set her hands on her hips. "You weren't torn between Christian and Riah. Riah was pining and you ignored him."

My skin pickled. Because I did suddenly understand what she was saying. "You think that's what's happening to these girls? That a dendrite is placing—" I shook my head. "*Planting* thoughts to get them on that paranormal forum and divert attention to the wolves so they can steal them away somewhere else?"

Aster stared at me for a beat. "Grace, I just want help with boys right now. I don't want to solve the world's problems." Glaring hard enough to make me wince, she spun on her heel and stalked away from us down the hall.

I bit my lip and looked to Stella.

"You are always trying to solve the world's problems," she said with a soft, encouraging smile.

Christian had a stupid grin on his face in siren skills. He had a stupid grin on his face and he was singing. Maribel had clearly said yes. But before I could congratulate him or tease him about his slicked back hair, Elbie's empty spot yawned at me.

I tried to ignore it, but every time I glanced back at Christian belting out the chorus, it tugged at my attention. Scowling as I leveled off a teaspoon of cinnamon and dumped it into a ball jar of silver sparkling siren tears, I said, "Are we going to have to rally behind Elbie and get him off the hook for taking Cora?"

Ethan snapped the back legs off a frog and passed it to Aster. "That depends on if you trust Sofia as an alibi."

Aster ripped the frog's head off and handed what was left of it back to Christian, then dropped the head in the jar. I shuddered as the siren tears churned the frog's milky eyes my way. "Sofia's many things, but she's not a liar."

I'm sorry about earlier, I apologized to Aster. Then, to everyone else, "I've actually recently begun to think a dendrite might be behind it."

Aster blew a kiss in my direction. "Have you dreamt anything, Chris? Any clues?"

"I don't know." His gaze flicked to mine, as I glanced over my shoulder. "I've just been dreaming about a basement. And Grace."

"Show us," Riah suggested. "Is it Ethan's basement?" Because I'd told Riah my theory in order to talk him down from feeling all protective.

"It's not Ethan's basement," Christian assured, as an image appeared, fully fleshed out, in my brain. Or, well, as fully fleshed out as Chris could pull it from his dream.

"What was that?" Nate asked, alarmed. The girl in the image was clearly me, sort of crumpled on the ground with a malformed, bloody lip.

"Is that a table in the background?" Riah asked.

"Looked like a corner to me," Ethan replied. "Hard to tell. Everything but Grace is shades of gray."

"Besides the steps."

"Yeah. They didn't look very safe. Think she fell?"

"What was that?" Nate repeated, eyes wide. He turned to me. "Grace..."

"He has portentous dreams," I explained. "They don't always pan out."

"They often do," Jeremy defended, his voice proud.

"They often mean at least something," Christian said absently, watching his frog mixture agitate in its glass. "Whether they tell the future, are just a warning, or stem from my fears..." He shrugged. It was an argument we'd had many times over. And this was him acknowledging I'd maybe been right and he should have done things differently at the end of our relationship.

I swallowed hard. "What do you think it means, that I'm the only one in the basement?" I hadn't really believed any of those girls had met up with some wolf, which meant I guess I'd been operating under the assumption that they were still out there somewhere. "Do you think it means they're gone?"

"Let's talk about the dance," Aster said, too brightly. "Instead of possibly dead classmates. I think we should all go together." Her gaze fluttered to Christian. "Maribel can come with."

"No." Riah turned in surprise. "I have plans."

Nate's attention swung swiftly to Aster. "You want to go as a group?"

"Well, I don't have a date, so yeah."

"What do you mean you don't have a date?" my cousin spit out on top of Jeremy's "You're not going with him?"

Aster flicked a look over her shoulder, past Nate and toward Jeremy. "He hasn't asked me."

Nathan stepped back to block their view of each other. "I didn't know I needed to. Aren't we dating?"

She sniffed. "I think you need to be dating exclusively to claim dance rights."

Jeremy was in front of her in a split vampire second. He took her hand and rubbed his thumb along it, clearing his throat. "Aster."

Nathan knocked our potion over, skillfully sending a stream of agitated frog brains directly into their clasped hands.

I huffed and yanked him out of the way, shoving him behind me. *Go,* I told him. *Get more tears.*

You get more tears.

I didn't knock it over. I pushed him into the aisle, opposite Aster and Jeremy. *Do it.*

He stalked to the front of the room while I wiped up the table and pulled what was left of the frog head out. Even with the tongs available, this still had me nearly retching. All I was able to take hold of was an eyeball, which wouldn't be enough. I sighed.

Jeremy took a deep breath. I'd never seen him so nervous. "Aster, would you go to the dance with me?"

"Yes, Jeremy, but..." She bit her lower lip and a long moment strung itself taut.

But what? I eventually asked Riah, Ethan, and Christian in my head.

Hold, please, Christian replied. *I'm busy watching a juicy drama play out. Anyone have some popcorn?*

"But what?" Jeremy asked quietly, concerned.

Nathan returned with a fresh jar of tears and tried to get back in between Aster and I, but I didn't let him.

"But I was thinking more for Grace's safety that we should go as a group. Under the circumstances."

Chapter Thirteen

Room Service

Now that there were three missing girls, the Sentinel could no longer write them off or ignore their parents' pleas to look into their disappearances. Not to mention the town's pleas. Enough feathers were ruffled that the town council had to do something. And since they insisted that the Sentinel was the new police, they had to let them act like police.

This meant, that with Sentinel resources, Justin was able to trace the IP address of the paranormal web forum in question to an address in the outskirts of Chicago. And with town council support, he was heading down to check it out.

When he offered to take me with, I jumped at the chance to visit some old friends—and bring my newer ones into normal-land for a trial run.

Aster slept over at my house the night before we left, Nora was parked out front when we woke up, and Riah arrived early enough for breakfast. Forty-five minutes later, we were still waiting on Christian.

Justin checked his phone, then motioned us all into his SUV. "He's not coming. Let's go."

"It's weird he hasn't texted me back," Aster said, as Clara put our bags in the trunk.

"Unless he slept in Iara," I pointed out, since you couldn't take your cell underwater.

"He definitely shouldn't have slept in Iara," Riah muttered. "Considering how late he and Maribel were out last night, there's no way he'd wake up on his own."

"Maybe he decided he couldn't leave her for two whole days," I said, crawling in the far back next to Riah. I wasn't being entirely sarcastic. He was kind of a hopeless romantic.

As predicted, Nora's nervous chatter increased the further we got from home. Thankfully, Clara was super patient with her and Justin answered all her questions, so I could relax. Or try to. I'd played it cool, that my friends would be fine in the big city, had reassured them time and again that pretending to be normal wasn't all that difficult, but the anxiety of how it would actually turn out was creeping in.

Aster napped, Nora eventually put her headphones on, and Riah ran his fingertip in patterns around my knee.

It was a four hour drive, so we stopped for food in Kohler and coffee in Kenosha. When we finally hit the city and could see skyscrapers from the highway, Nora sat up, Riah stopped his swirling, Aster stopped dozing, and Clara's mouth hung open.

Justin caught my eye in the rearview mirror and winked.

"Looks like I'll take them through the city then? Instead of around?"

I tried to smile but three and a half years ago, we'd been run out of this city by a small Hand of Humanity cell. The thought of getting anywhere near our old neighborhood had me on high alert. *Mom made us promise to not get too close,* I reminded him.

We're past Lincoln Park already. And in a new car. You're not on their radar anymore, trust me.

I slid my hand into Riah's and rested my chin on his shoulder as my brother headed straight into downtown Chicago. When he drove past The Bean, he said, "This is as much tourism as you're going to get, so soak it in."

He was planning to dump us at the hotel so he and Clara could head out to investigate. My parents were not happy about them poking around, considering neither of them had any actual training, but they all tried not to talk about it, lest it turn into an argument about what qualifications a Sentinel should have and whether or not it was a good idea for my brother to stay with them as a career.

He usually shut them up by pointing out that if there weren't any old Shady on the Sentinel, the town would be in even more trouble. And anyway, he had Ethan's uncle on speed dial. Justin and Clara were working this Chicago address for both the Sentinel and the currently underground police force. Picked by the first because we'd lived there and he knew the area, and by the latter because he was their mole.

Honestly, at this point, Officer Parrino was directing every move Justin made, which was a pretty good education if you asked me.

Riah's mouth was hanging open now too, his nose nearly pressed against the window.

You're too cute, I told him.

He peeled his attention away from the city and kissed me once. "This is when you realize I'm just a small town boy from Wisconsin."

Well, don't worry. You don't look like a small town boy from Wisconsin.

He gathered a smirk. "What do I look like?"

My eyes widened as I realized, "You look like something Rea is going to eat right up." Charlie, Rea, and Lucia were meeting us for lunch. They were the test for those of us in the car who were here to get a taste of normal. "I should warn you, she can't really talk to a hot guy without throwing herself at him."

"Even if he's completely into someone else?" There was a deep, intimate channel to his tone that flipped my stomach. I tried to remember I was in the car with my brother and we probably should choose another location to make out.

"Even then," I muttered.

Riah looked back out his window. Right. The tour wasn't over.

"I got ahold of Jeremy," Aster said brightly. "He's meeting Chris later and promised to tease him incessantly for us."

— ✧ —

My brother stalked out of the hotel and doled out our room keys.

"Two for you," to Nora and Aster, "one for you," to Clara, "and two for you," to Riah and I.

I stared at him. Justin grabbed my arm and pulled me out of sight of the others, behind the car, then offered me three condoms I didn't take. Gaping at them, I about choked on my own spit.

"I thought I was staying with you and Clara?" I whisper-cried. "Didn't mom get one room with a pullout couch?"

He snorted. "Yeah, no." *Do we need to have the talk?*

What talk?

The birds and the bees talk.

Of course we don't need to have the talk!

You've had it with mom?

Yes!

You on birth control?

No!

Then take these. He shoved the condoms into my hand.

Justin! I'm not having this conversation with you!

He frowned. *Then you're probably not ready to have sex.*

I never said I was! Was I? I hadn't thought about it.

So you and Christian never...

I shook my head, beet red, I was sure, and completely morti-fied.

Huh. I was sure that's why it took him so long to get over you. He snapped his fingers. *Bet that's why Christian bailed. Didn't want to share a room with the two of you and have to see that.*

You think I'd have had sex with Riah in the same room as my ex-boyfriend?

He shrugged. *Be safe, okay?* Then he was gone around the other side of the car, leading everyone into the hotel. He and Clara had to dump her blood in the mini-fridge before they left and then we were on our own.

I swallowed.

Stella and Ethan had sex, and Aster and Kevin had done everything but. I'd just never been so deep in before that anything nudged me in that direction. My hormones hadn't woken up maybe, or I hadn't been comfortable enough with Christian, no matter how much I liked him. He'd been jealous, and instead of that making me want to prove anything to him, it only made me want to turn away.

Riah rounded the car. "You coming?"

I stared at him, still slightly dumbfounded, the condoms now hanging out of my hand. "We've only been official for a few months," I muttered. "Are we even official?"

His brow furrowed as he took a complete assessment, eyes landing eventually on the items in my hand, to which he raised his eyebrows. "Your brother gave you those?"

I only had it in me to blink.

"Nice to know we have his approval, I guess."

Did that mean he was in?

I was so stupid. Of course he was in.

Shaking my head, I brushed past him and walked through the hotel with a handful of condoms and a backpack slung over my shoulder.

⁓ℓℓ⁓

"Nora, Aster, Riah, this is Charlie, Rea, and Lucia." The seven of us stood awkwardly in a circle in the lobby.

Charlie curtsied and smirked at Riah, since they'd met before and had more than a few conversations over the years. He gave her a lopsided smile back and pulled her into a hug.

Rea zoned in on Riah's backside. "Do I get one of those?"

"A Riah or a hug?" Charlie asked with a laugh.

"Either." Rea's smile was shy, as if she were anything of the sort. She was a big talker, and a bigger flirt, and she had been since any of us could remember.

Lucia pushed her in my direction. "From Grace, you get a hug." Then to me, she asked, "Did you warn him about her?"

"Let's play spin the bottle," Rea suggested, clapping her hands together.

"Good thing you warned *me*," Aster muttered. "Or I might rip her throat out."

"That's... violent." Charlie carefully reassessed the little wolf standing next to me.

Ripping a throat out is a very flippant wolf thing to say, I explained. *Not so flippant to a human. Might need to tone it down a bit.*

Aster beamed at Charlie. "Kidding. Let's order pizza." She side-eyed Rea before leading Charlie off to discuss the dinner order without consulting anyone else. Which sounded about right.

Rea took Lucia in one arm and Riah in the other to follow Charlie and Aster. "Okay, so you and Grace," she cooed. "I do know you're together. And I love her. But I'd still like to appreciate you while you're here, if you don't mind."

"When she says appreciate, she doesn't mean anything inappropriate," Lucia quickly explained. "We've trained her out of that."

He looked over his shoulder at me.

I'll be right there. Had to take care of Nora first. She might as well have been frozen in her spot. I couldn't even tell if she was breathing or not.

"Nora, Lucia is a diver."

"A diver? What's that?"

"Swim and dive?" I explained. *Like, diving into water. Water, because you're a siren and you like to swim and dive too?*

"Oh! Right. I love to dive. Diving is the best. Being in the water..." Nora rolled her eyes up to the ceiling in what could only be described as...

"*Ecstasy,*" Rea emphasized in her conversation with Riah.

Relax, I told Nora. *They don't bite, remember? We're the ones who bite.*

She nodded profusely as we made our way over to the sitting area. Riah had chosen a chair and Rea was sitting on the arm of it. He grabbed my waist and pulled me down on his lap. It had been a bit of a panicked werewolf yank, judging by how hard I'd landed.

"Oh," Rea muttered, setting a hand on his bicep. "Stronger than he looks too."

Wrapping his arms around me, Riah curled himself along my back. I recognized he was hiding from her more than anything, but all I could think about were the condoms I'd tossed on the bedside table. And why I'd tossed them there instead of by the TV. What kind of subliminal message did that send, within reach versus across the room where he'd have to get up to get them.

I must have flushed red because Aster and Charlie, who'd had their heads tucked together working on the pizza order across from us, looked up at once. Aster no doubt smelled me, and Charlie had a sixth sense about when a tone in the room changed.

They both gave me questioning looks. My old best friend and my new. I had to clamp myself down from sending them the same response in their head, and directed it to Aster only. *My brother gave me condoms for tonight.*

Her eyes went wide and then she burst into laughter. Everyone looked at her.

"Sorry, it was just something—"

Nope, I warned. *You do not say it was something I said in your head.* This was exactly what we were practicing for.

She bit her lip and shrugged. "I'm prone to fits of laughter. It's a quirk."

Right, I said to Aster, Nora, and Riah, *so you're going to have to get better about not responding to what I say in your head.*

Aster gave me a petulant look, as if maybe I could stop talking in her head in the first place.

Fair enough.

~ele~

After pizza, we went back to our respective rooms to change into our swimsuits.

Riah caught me around the waist before the door even closed all the way and buried his face in my neck. "Save me from her. You must save me."

I laughed, but it came out like I was choking. Because everything Rea said about his arms and abs and chest and hands were true. And suddenly, between the condoms and Rea referring to him as a lollipop, my awareness of Riah and our physical relationship was at an all-time high.

Honestly, I hadn't gotten around to thinking about it before today. And being that I operated on brain power first and foremost, I needed the time to overthink this. Time I didn't have if we were going to use one of those condoms.

Then I was kissing him, my hands sliding up his shirt and fingertips sparking. The electricity danced across his skin, causing him to shudder against me, which did not have a cooling effect. One of his hands held us tight, hip to hip, and the other had snuck under my shirt to loop a finger around the side band of my bra.

"Sorry." He let go and stepped away. "I'm so sorry."

I tried to calm my breathing, because wow. That had gone

142

somewhere fast. "Sorry?"

"I know you're not ready."

Because he could smell me. Of course.

"I just... got a little carried away." He ran a hand through his hair and *my word* he was gorgeous. Rea was right; he was wasted on me.

"No, I'm sorry."

"Grace, you have nothing to be sorry about."

"You're ready, though."

"So? What does that matter?"

I thought about this, but didn't have an answer. I wasn't going to apologize for not being ready, even if he was. But I was sorry we weren't at the same place. Sorry I hadn't thought about it. I should have.

"Just so we're clear," he said, "we're talking about ordering room service, right?"

I laughed. And stepped back into him. And ran my hands up and into his hair. "I do want you," I whispered.

"I know," he whispered. "I can smell it. That's exactly what I got a little carried away with."

I smiled, breathing him in. "And this whole time, you've been careful with me because you can also smell my reservation?" It hurt my heart to think he felt like that. That I had reservations.

"It doesn't smell like reservation. It smells like fear." He put his hands on my face and tilted my head up to look at him. "But you're not afraid of me, right?"

Honestly, I think I was afraid of the responsibility. Sex meant babies and STDs, even though I knew neither of us had any previous partners and that we were both the type to be safe. I was also afraid of the intimacy, like falling deep into a hole with someone you could never fully shake after. There was an innate commitment in that to me, unveiling myself completely and letting him all the way in. Unpopular opinion, but, "Doesn't it make a tiny bit of sense to save one thing to share with only one person?"

"Sure it does."

"But that's not how you feel?"

"I don't see there being another person for me after you." But he smirked when he said it, then tugged me down on the bed next to him.

We sat facing the condoms and I sighed.

"I want to share this with you—when you're ready," he continued. "Because I'm in for whatever's in store for us, all the way, as long as it lasts. Because I can't imagine caring about anyone more. But if I do, or if you do, or if shit happens, at least I can look back knowing I gave you my all and my everything while I had you."

I blinked back tears because that was the most beautiful thing anyone had ever said to me. "Well, if that doesn't make me want to take you right here, right now."

He laughed and stood. "I'm gonna make it easy for you and take it off the table."

"No room service?" I cocked my head. "You're taking room service off the table?"

Grabbing the condoms, he went to the bathroom and tossed them in the trash as someone started pounding on the door. Riah opened it on Aster and Nora, who were dressed for the pool, but something was wrong. They both looked wrong.

"Chris stood Jeremy up too," Aster said. "I'm worried now."

"Worried about what?" Riah asked.

"He's a dendrite," she said, sweeping into the room. "And he's missing."

"He's not a girl, though," I pointed out.

"Maybe it's not about being a girl," Aster snapped.

"Riah, text your sister." And I grabbed my phone to text his parents.

A few minutes of Aster pacing later and the responses were in:

From Maribel: **don't be a dick riah ik he's with you**

From Christian's mom: **He's not in Chicago with you?**

From Charlie: **what's taking you guys so long?**

Chapter Fourteen

Call the Sentinel

I couldn't get a hold of Justin, and when I finally did, he scolded me for blowing up his phone during an investigation. When I told him what had happened, he said it would be far more useful for Christian if he finished what he was doing and got some answers.

Aster decided it best if we pretended everything was normal and met Charlie, Lucia, and Rea in the pool as planned. But Charlie could tell I was upset, and when she heard Christian was missing, she got out of the pool and toweled off, said she'd drop Lucia and Rea at home and drive us back to Shady herself if Justin wouldn't.

Which we couldn't let happen, of course, considering how poorly the first time she'd been in Shady had gone.

I begged Nora to charm the worry off us, and we played it like Aster had finally gotten a text from Christian. Problem solved. Once we were back in our room, though, I paced most of the night while Riah tapped the remote against his palm. He flipped maniacally through the channels as if anything from Shady might actually show up on the screen and texted intermittently with Maribel.

Sometime after midnight, when I started crying about what a shit I was, that I should have cared this much when Jess and Sasha and Cora went missing, Riah crawled to the end of the bed and caught me in his arms.

"Of course it didn't feel the same," he said, looking up at me. "You didn't know them enough to feel certain they wouldn't disappear on their own. There was a level of doubt. With Christian, you... know him."

"Still, we should have done something."

"What could we have done?"

It was a question I spent the entire next day and night considering: What could we do?

There was no point going to the Sentinel. They were doing what they would, which was let Justin and Clara head the investigation.

And there was no point going to the police. They were doing what they could too, which was help from behind the scenes.

No point going to Justin and Clara. They'd dropped us in Shady and headed straight for Green Bay. The lady in Chicago who started the forum said a guy in Green Bay had hired her to set it up.

By the time Monday morning rolled around, I was easily agitated and chomping at the bit. It occurred to me, as soon as I laid eyes on Sofia at school, that maybe she'd done something to Christian in order to get Elbie released, same as Elbie had done for Nehemiah last year.

The accusation was half out of my mouth when Aster pointed out that Christian was literally the last person Sofia would terrorize. She could have accomplished the same thing with anyone else.

I slumped down in class, not bothering to take notes. That's how terrible my focus was. Or maybe how completely it was set on Christian and who he might have gone with willingly. He'd dropped Maribel off and driven home. Or, at least, his car had made it home. He'd parked on the street, which he only did when he wanted to play basketball, but his mom didn't let him play after dark—didn't want it bothering the neighbors who might be trying to sleep. The only thing that made sense was if someone had been waiting for him. Someone he knew and trusted, because there'd been no sign of a struggle. Someone who might have convinced him to come with them.

Convinced. Which brought me back to Aster asking if placed thoughts could grow. If such a thing *was* possible, then someone could do the prep work and not actually have to be there when those girls walked out under the full moon. Or maybe it had never about the full moon in the first place. If the planter directed them somewhere else, maybe the website was only a smoke screen to throw blame.

The idea of such control being wielded over another person made it almost difficult to breathe.

Control. What had Nate said about preferring to live normal? That no one there could control him? I'd thought he was being dramatic, but if he was really worried about that, it was because he knew how to do it or because it had been done to him.

"Jer?" I asked, as we walked out of Spanish. "Have you ever heard of people growing thoughts? You know, like, mind control?"

"Sure. It's not unheard of. Not easy, though, and not generally worth it. Chris... would... he'd..." His words slowed and skipped as he turned to me. "He'd know better than me. I was gonna tell you to ask him." We stopped in the middle of the hall where we generally parted. Throngs bustled around us. "When he first started having his dreams, his dad looked into whether it might be an effect of someone planting thoughts."

"I feel like, under the circumstances, I shouldn't ask his dad."

"I feel like, under the circumstances, that's a good call. What about your uncle?"

I nodded. In addition to being the school's math teacher, he was also the skills instructor. That did make the most sense.

Settling in quietly next to Aster and Nora in calc, I watched him scurry around the room in front of me. He seemed older than his years, and crooked. Crooked teeth, crooked smile, crooked posture, crooked hair. Even his shirt was buttoned wrong today, one off. Maybe I'd pop in after school and see what he knew about it.

Nora opened her mouth, but Aster stopped her with a look. Neither of us wanted to talk. About anything. We were somber, waiting for news, waiting for Christian to walk into school like nothing had happened. Like his parents hadn't spent all yesterday combing town for him.

I stared at the board until it was blurry, till all I could see were the thoughts in my brain.

No drained bodies had been found, no bones, no trace of a full moon gone bad. So was there a dendrite out there controlling minds, as dangerous as any wild, blood-thirsty wolf or vampire?

Walking into the lunchroom, I searched the crowd for anyone I might consider creepy enough or charming enough to do something like this. Not that it couldn't be someone outside the school, or an adult. That probably made more sense—if you knew how to plant thoughts and make them grow, you'd probably have to be an adult.

Nate scraped his chair back and sat down for lunch.

Nate.

Nathan.

The one who'd originally mentioned mind control.

"Is growing thoughts a real thing?" I asked him, holding back my lunch until he gave me an answer.

"Your parents never try to push you in one direction or another?"

"All parents do that."

"Yeah, well, dendrite parents have more skills to actually force the issue."

"My parents would never use their abilities to sway me. Never." They might have kept secrets from me, but this, I knew, they would never do.

He shrugged and tried to get at my lunch.

"Nate." I shifted in my chair, tucking the bag under my arm. "What does your dad make you do?"

He scowled and looked away, his eyes landing for only a second on Christian's chair.

I have a thing for dendrites, he'd said. This memory had me nearly choking. Sensing my weakness, he took my lunch and fished the sandwich out of it.

He sensed my weakness.

Could this be why they moved so much, because my cousin was a predator?

But then what did Christian have to do with it?

I waited until he was done with the sandwich, then held my orange out to him. When he went to take it, I asked, "Do you like guys?"

He snorted, his hand coming down on the orange. "Are you asking if I'm bi?"

"Yes."

He frowned. "No."

"What does that mean?"

"What does 'no' mean? No means no, Grace." And his frown morphed into a smirk.

Creepy and charming, both.

I let go of the orange. Our lunch table was mostly quiet; conversation spattered across the table in short, unenthusiastic bursts. Christian had been sitting with Maribel lately, but even so, his empty chair felt bigger than the rest of us.

There was something about my cousin, something that I'd explained away because of his night terrors and the trauma of finding his mom. Add to that someone controlling his mind at some point or another and it could definitely mold him into a predator. But wouldn't we have noticed something? He was with us most of the time. He didn't have any other friends. I mean, he went to his dad's parties, which we didn't go to, but...

But Christian hadn't gone to his parties either.

If it was Nate, Christian didn't make sense.

Psychology held me, purely because we were studying Antisocial Personality Disorder.

Sense of entitlement, check. Unremorseful, check. Apathetic to others, check. Manipulative and cunning, check. Affectively cold, check. Socially irresponsible, check. Six out of twelve wasn't bad.

Or maybe I should say it wasn't good.

Could my cousin be a sociopath?

I considered his egocentricity, callousness, lack of conscience, inability to resist temptation, tendency to be antagonistic, deprecating attitude toward the opposite sex, and lack of interest in bonding to a mate.

Perhaps.

Could you push me so far to think he might be a psychopath?

I could hardly bring myself to look at the list: glib and superficial charm, need for stimulation, manipulative, grandiose sense of self-worth, pathological lying, lack of remorse or guilt, shallow affect, callousness and lack of empathy, parasitic lifestyle, poor behavioral controls, early behavior problems, lack of realistic long-term goals, impulsivity, irresponsibility, and failure to accept responsibility for own actions.

Well, it certainly wasn't all off.

I shut my book with a whimper.

If Nate was behind this, I was safe and Christian's dream was wrong. If he wasn't, maybe the one thing I could do was put myself in the path of whoever it actually was. I was, after all, a dendrite and a girl—aside from Chris, that was who'd gone missing. And I was trained up to defend myself.

Christian's dream had me suffering from a bloody lip, which seemed manageable. I'd almost worked out my plan when I got a text from my brother.

its dads old place

where he grew up

guy said he just rented it a few months ago but grace

its owned by a george jameson

george is dead but he owns two properties in shady

get riah to town hall asap and have him find out which ones

I stared at the screen, limbs heavy with what he was telling me, my last illusions shattered.

A dendrite *could* be as much of a monster as anyone else. And not only that, but there was a monster in my very own family.

calling the cops to have them come out here and see if I missed something

no, I replied.

call the sentinel

easier for them to get out of town

and then I can call the cops when I need them

instead of having to call the sentinel

what?

no

what are you planning?

Grace

GRACE

just call the sentinel justin

trust me

Chapter Fifteen

It Hadn't Been a Wolf

I explained the plan to Riah, Ethan, Stella, Aster, and Jeremy during the seven minutes between classes.

Phase one was Aster trying to get Nathan to do something with her after school. She attempted this in siren skills, but he refused, salty that she'd rushed to Jeremy when we got home from Chicago the night before. Of course she'd rushed to Jeremy, she said, his best friend was missing.

I'd never heard her whine so good.

It didn't work.

When the final bell rang, she came with me and Riah to town hall for phase two. It took him seventeen minutes to pull up the property tax files and print out the addresses owned by the late George Jameson.

One was the house I'd spent Christmas in.

The second was a property supposedly nestled behind it.

Both street numbers corresponded to marked pages in my dad's bible.

I pulled out of the parking lot and headed to the first address, as Riah texted Ethan the second.

Phase three was Ethan, Stella, and hopefully Sergeant Parrino checking out this second property while the three of us headed to my cousin's on the pretense of paying him a social visit. We were assuming that the basement in Christian's dream—the basement where we suspected the girls had ended up—wasn't in the house they lived in, since they had people over all the time. So, our plan was to keep Nathan distracted and in sight while the cops hopefully found Christian, Jess, Sasha, and Cora.

Jeremy was making his way there on foot to meet us, not only because he was fast like that, but also in case we needed the element of surprise.

When we neared the property, I slowed to forty-five miles per hour. There weren't speed limits in Shady Woods, but forty-five felt sure and steady. The right speed for a casual visit to a friend's house. I pulled up in the gravel driveway and parked next to my uncle's car, coming to a stop with a crunch. There had been a ton of snow for Christmas, but it had all melted out within the last few weeks.

I led the way, something we'd argued about the entire drive there. Apparently, my wolves still saw me as the weakest link, but if we needed to play this off like we were worried about my cousin, I would logically be the one in front. And they might be stronger, but I was more stubborn and had arguably more training. They were the ones who'd trained me, sure, but at this point I'd been trained by four different people. Aster's dad had taught her self-defense, but other than that, they fought only on instinct.

Riah was so close behind me, ready to pull me out of danger at the slightest wink of it, that I kept stumbling from his toes on my heels. I stopped to give him a look. He gave me one back.

With a huff, I knocked on the door, switched feet, and knocked again. Aster, impatient, rang the doorbell. Riah peeked in the window, then looked to us and shook his head.

Okay, well, I was family, right? I tried the doorknob and it gave.

"Nathan!" Aster cried, stepping in front of me over the threshold. "Nathan, are you here?"

Riah motioned for me to follow her, finally giving me some space now that Aster had managed to weasel her way in front of me.

"Uncle Rich?"

Aster took the stairs, calling for Nathan as she moved from room to room up there, and I wandered the main level.

This was stupid. We were definitely no longer acting normal.

Riah checked the basement and we all met back up in the hall.

"Not a soul," Aster muttered.

"And not a creepy basement," Riah reported.

But the car. That car in the driveway meant they were here. Or, I supposed, they could be at this property number two. On the plat map, it didn't look to be too far a walk. Even so, we'd never seen it. Aster and my grandparents lived out in this area, and none of us could picture it. We couldn't even picture a driveway that might lead to it.

I strode to the back door. The storm was wide open, the screen the only barrier between us and the rest of the world. Not something you do mid-winter in the Northwoods of Wisconsin.

Stepping outside, I studied the smooth path that led from the steps into the woods. As if someone had shoveled it regularly before it melted down. We stood quietly and still for a good handful of minutes before I took a deep breath and stepped down onto it.

Jeremy slipped out from behind a fat trunk, quiet as a mouse. "May I?" he asked.

I nodded. With his vampire hearing, he could map the area ahead of him in a way we couldn't, which meant he'd know exactly what we were stepping into.

Grabbing the back of his coat, I followed close behind. It was a thin straggle of a path as we entered the woods, so Riah did the same to me and Aster came last. We walked for maybe five minutes before Jeremy stopped, opened his eyes, and motioned me forward.

Ducking into the underbrush, I inched closer, ignoring the flashes that brought me back to Mr. Turner last year, when I'd found him in the woods. Pray God this wouldn't end up the same as that had.

Even here, even with this sort of proof, I held back the sway of my panic with the hope that it wouldn't be Nathan I found over Christian in a basement.

An old farmhouse came into view, its weathered wood clinging to a frame that might as well have died off years ago. Windows were broken, awnings awry, and the lawn was so long it had folded over in dead winter clumps.

I stumbled. This was the house in my dad's picture. The one with the family tucked into the pages of Ruth.

My cousin sat on the back steps, leaning forward a little, elbows on his knees, hands clasped where they hung in front of him. His face was blank, as if his soul had been removed from him and hung up somewhere else.

It wasn't the look of someone wreaking all this havoc, but the face of someone being controlled. Of someone who'd given up fighting.

As if he could sense me, he looked up.

I do what he says. The memory of that first night at our house rose up in my mind, so faint I almost couldn't catch it.

What are you doing? I asked, as if that wasn't a better question for him to be asking us.

Waiting for Rich. What are you doing?

Looking for Christian.

You think you'll find him? He asked this casually.

You don't?

I try not to think too much about it.

He stood and I moved out from under the tree cover. The others followed. As if I'd asked him to bring me to Christian,

Nate headed around the house to where the address still hung aside a propped open front door. Propped open because it had fallen from one of its hinges. Inside was more of the same: a collection of rotten floorboards, some ancient chairs weak with holes, and a kitchen gaping empty of appliances. There, Nate stopped in front of a door that held a shiny new knob.

I tried it, but this one didn't give.

Moving me aside, Aster shoved her foot into the door, right beneath the knob, and it splintered enough to swing open on a black cavity yawning below. I felt for a light switch but it did nothing. Jeremy in the lead, we headed down stairs that seemed to shift with every step. At the bottom, he disappeared into the void and soon the room began to pop with light.

Jeremy walked the perimeter, flipping on battery-operated wall sconces one by one. I looked around as the lights slowly revealed a spotless workroom. A desk and chair. A machine hooked up to a helmet. A massage table with a little wheely stand that held a tray full of instruments.

Aster gasped, then ran over to the corner where Christian was strapped to a chair, and limp. She dropped to her knees in front of him, and I rushed over, calling his name, in and out of his head. His only response was an unintelligible murmur that barely tickled my mind. I pulled at the tethers, a motion that seemed to shake Aster from her shock, and she snapped them apart with her hands.

"Oh my God, Nathan," I whispered breathlessly, tears filling my eyes as I stumbled back. "What has he done?"

Jeremy swooped in to check Christian's pulse as if he might not have one. But he wasn't dead. He was a distant murmur in my head, as if he knew we were here and was trying to communicate.

I spun on my cousin, whose attention was fixed on the floor. "What did he do? Stop it! Undo it!" When he didn't answer, I shoved at one of his shoulders.

"He's trying to fix them." He glanced up at me, then stared at Christian. "The normals, anyway. He learns on us so he can fix normals. I mean, he's trying."

"What do you mean he's trying?" I whimpered. "What's wrong with Christian?"

"Christian's drugged," Aster said softly. "Right?" She looked to Riah, who nodded. They must be able to smell it.

I turned back to my cousin. "Why's he drugged?"

He threw up his arms. "Probably so he doesn't fight back."

"Fight back when what?" I demanded. "What do you mean, learns on them? He can't learn anything from Christian. He can't make anyone have dreams like Christian does. That's the siren in him. A once in a lifetime mix of his siren and dendrite genes and nothing that will show up in his brain."

"I'm sorry," he muttered. "I tried to stop him."

"Tried to stop him?!" I stormed. "Tried to stop him today? Tried to stop him from taking Christian? Jess? Tried to stop him years ago? How long has this been going on? And he's still *trying*? How long before you realize abnormals can't be *made* and you stop helping a *monster*?"

Nate shut his eyes tight and Riah stepped up next to me, as if he was with me, whatever I decided to do next. As if he'd tear my cousin apart if I moved in that direction.

"Which would you like me to answer first?" But this was Rich's voice, from the top of the stairs.

We all froze as he shuffled slowly down them.

"He tried to stop me when I was working on his mother, but his help made things end poorly, so he's been more cooperative since." My uncle took a few steps toward us. "He tried to stop me from taking Christian, but a boy with portentous dreams able to see into my workspace poses a threat."

Nate moved toward the scalpels, and I wondered how likely it might be that he was arming himself to help us, but he only picked one up to press the blade against his thumb. Blood dribbled down it, bright and red, to make a little pool on the tray.

His mother. Head smashed in like a wolf had gotten her, he'd said. Only, it hadn't been a wolf.

Horror flooded through me—did Nate realize it hadn't been a wolf?—and I turned back to my uncle. "You killed your wife."

"I didn't kill her," he snapped. "I was fixing her. I thought... I was sure it was going to work that time. *He* killed her."

Nate squeezed his eyes shut tight again and squeezed harder on the blade. I shuddered, but I couldn't worry about him right now. I couldn't lose my focus. It might be four against two, or even five against one, but my uncle couldn't, at this point, let us out of here alive if he wanted to come out unscathed himself. As much as I wanted to rush over to my cousin and rip that scalpel out of his hand, tell him it was okay and *not his fault*—he most certainly had not killed his mother—I couldn't risk it.

"Are they dead?"

"Who?" my uncle asked absently. Rich. Rich asked absently. Was this why Nate couldn't call him dad? Because it made his stomach turn? Putting a hand to my belly, I tried to keep the nausea in.

"The rest of them," Aster spat. "Jess. Sasha. Cora."

"Oh yes. Well, if I were able to conduct my research in a better facility, their recovery would be easier. As it is, I can't really have them leading anyone back to me, can I?"

Now *that* was indeed antisocial, sociopathic, and psychotic behavior. I folded over and held my knees to keep the dizziness at bay. This was my blood, my father's brother. His evil ran in my veins.

In a flash, my uncle charged for Riah, who crumpled immediately to the ground. Aster launched herself at Rich in response, and that was when I saw the needles in my uncle's hands. Too late to warn her, she fell into a heap next to Riah as two syringes clattered to the cement.

I nearly threw myself on top of them with a wail, but Jeremy was beside me in a vampire second. Gripping my arm, he positioned us in front of our unconscious friends, pushing my uncle back.

"Nathan," Rich ordered, as he took stock of us. "Go upstairs."

My cousin took a step toward the stairs.

"No, Nate. Help us." We only had to hold out until Stella and Ethan got here with backup.

Nate paused.

"Do as I say." Rich's voice held a heady weight.

"No! You don't own him!"

Nate looked between us.

"In order to control a mind," my uncle said, "the victim must love the person, or think they love them, or at the very least *believe* in them. There must be an open, willing channel. Tell me, Grace, do you really think Nathan loves you more than he loves me?"

"Why are you doing this?" I asked.

He studied Jeremy as he answered, "So everyone can be special."

"Turn them, then. Making a human a vampire or wolf is easier than brain surgery." As if Samuel had reached into my soul and spoken through me, from wherever he was. "Are you working for Samuel?"

"Who's Samuel?" He and Jeremy were facing each other now, and Jeremy readied himself the way he used to when we'd spar.

"No one," I muttered, trying to think of a way to split my uncle's focus and give Jeremy the upper hand. "Well, someone who could've helped Grace, maybe."

Damn if I didn't keep siding with Samuel in all this.

My uncle's shoulders sagged and I won his attention with that. "I could have fixed her, if he hadn't stopped me."

The facts clicked into place and I stumbled back. "*You* killed your sister?" It wasn't that our grandpa was protecting the dendrite secret, or the town... It was that he had been protecting Rich.

"You have to understand, I would have fixed her. He found us and started yelling about her head being split open, but it wasn't. It was carefully pulled apart. I could have fixed it. I could have put her back together, I—"

Jeremy charged him like a bull. They landed near the rolling table of instruments, and my uncle yanked one of its legs to send it tumbling. He scrambled for the nearest scalpel and sliced Jeremy's gut wide open.

Nathan, who'd been holding onto the splintered banister so tight his knuckles were white, took off up the stairs.

Jeremy dropped to his elbow, then fell onto his back, hands cupped over the oozing.

Now would be good, I told Stella and Ethan, wherever they were, as my uncle stalked toward me, bloody scalpel in hand. *Now would be very good.*

Chapter Sixteen

You Hurt Him Just Right

"How do you suppose you're going to get out of this?" I asked my uncle, before dropping to my knees and sliding beneath the outstretched arm he'd planned to scalpel me with.

Coming back up onto my feet as gracefully as when I'd practiced it, I found myself right where I wanted to be at the base of the stairs.

He spun around to find where I'd gone, his nostrils flared and sneer vicious. I didn't have a weapon on me, but I had skill and training and a hard wooden banister. It seemed that he was out of needles, so as long as I could avoid the scalpel, I should be fine. I'd taken some hits during training, and couldn't imagine that fighting a dendrite would be more difficult than the vampires and wolves I'd managed to best before.

"You plan to leave us all here, half unconscious, and make it out of town before anyone can find you? Leave Nate to take the fall? What?"

When he came at me next, I took one step over, catching the wrist he was planning to knife me with in one hand and his neck in the other, then slammed his face into the end of the banister.

The hit made a resounding crack, and he fell with the thud of body knocked out.

The sound shuddered through me—the fact that I'd knocked someone out shuddered through me.

Scrambling backward, up the stairs to get some distance, I landed hard on a step that groaned with my weight but held beneath me.

When I registered the pool of blood seeping from Rich's head wound, the despair and horror gutted me. I searched out Jeremy in the shadows behind the overturned table. "Is he dead?"

"I don't know," he replied. His breathing was labored and one hand clutched his stomach while the other, propped behind him, held him upright. "But I taught you well." And he eked out a thin smile.

Minutes ticked by, an expanse of time that felt like hours, before footsteps sounded above us. Stella led the way, then Ethan and his uncle with a handful of other cops in tow.

By the time they hauled Christian, Riah, Aster, Jeremy, and my uncle up the stairs, Nate was nowhere to be found. Rich was awake enough to slap the paramedics away but not with it enough to put up any real fight, which was more than I could say for my friends.

They were all headed to town for Dr. Riley's clinic, but Jeremy and I were stuck behind, the only ones left to give a statement while it was still fresh in our minds. We sat in separate squad cars, me with Officer Andres and Jeremy with Officer Brabant. Someone had sourced him siren tears for his belly, which had already begun to heal on its own by the time we'd made it up the stairs and out of the house.

I left Nate out of my story, knowing full well that Jeremy might not leave him out of his. It was clear that Rich had manipulated my cousin, coerced him, *controlled* him, and I hoped Jeremy could see that too. If he didn't, it was something I'd deal with later. Maybe I'd blame my omission on the squad car's radio, which was calling in volunteer firefighters to walk the property and look for bodies.

Bodies.

Because that was a distraction if I'd ever heard of one.

After we finished, as Officer Andres drove us to my car, we passed the Sentinel's trucks. She glanced over at me. "I'm glad we got you guys out of there when we did."

When Jeremy and I walked into the clinic, the receptionist, having worked for Christian's dad her entire career, knew exactly who we were.

She led us to the patient rooms and pointed to the first closed door. "Christian's awake. The other two will be fine, but they aren't conscious yet."

"And my... Rich?"

"What, honey?"

"There was a fourth patient. An adult male. He had a head wound."

Her expression creased in concern like I might be losing it. "I don't think that's right, dear."

"It is right. I—"

Jeremy slipped his hand through mine and squeezed. "Let's see Chris, yeah? We can worry about Mr. Jameson later."

"What if he... did I not hurt him enough?" I whispered. "Did I hurt him too much?"

"From what I saw, you hurt him just right." Opening the door, he tugged me inside.

Christian was sitting up in bed, hooked to an IV and on his cell. He smiled at us, as brilliantly as the first day I'd met him.

I leaned over to give him a hug, a nugget of unease settling deep in my gut. What had happened to my uncle?

Jeremy swallowed us both with his long arms, trapping me there for a minute. As we straightened, he asked Christian if he was okay.

"Seems that way. What about you? I might have been trapped in my brain, but I saw you got your middle split open."

Spreading his arms to reveal the spread of deep purple vampire blood soaked into his shirt, he then lifted the hem so we could see how his skin was knitting the last layer of itself back together.

Christian turned a soft smile my way. "And there she was, in the basement, just like I said she would be."

"Saving the day," Jeremy added. He leaned toward Christian and whispered, "I taught her that."

"Saving me," Christian corrected. "Should've known you wouldn't be the victim, but the savior."

I made a face, but on the inside, my stomach turned. Did saviors kill people? What had happened to my uncle?

The door opened and an officer stuck his head in. "Sorry to interrupt, but I heard you were awake. I'd really like to talk to you as soon as possible."

"Sure." Christian nodded. "Come on in."

He took the stool and flipped open his notebook. "Alone perhaps?"

"Right." Jeremy took my hand from Christian's and pulled me into the hall, shutting the door behind us.

Maribel came running around the corner, sliding to a stop in front of me. "Is he in there?"

"Riah? No, that's Christian."

"Riah? No. Christian called when he got here. What do you mean Riah?"

"He'll be fine," Jeremy cooed. "Everyone's fine."

"An officer is taking his statement," I said. "He requested privacy."

She nodded, out of breath, and settled cross-legged on the floor. "Okay, I'll wait."

Jeremy pushed open the next door to reveal Aster, skin unnaturally pale and dark curls splayed across the white pillowcase. He slipped inside.

Dr. Riley came around the corner and headed for the third door. I followed him.

"What did he do to them?" I asked, stopping at the foot of Riah's bed to stare at his slack face.

"It was a disabling cocktail. A sedative that also knocks out any abilities lurking under the surface. It's usually used for dendrites, as our brains sometimes keep working after our bodies are impaired." He checked Riah's leads and the amount of IV fluid that was left.

Sitting down in the chair next to Riah, I took his hand in mine. "How long before he wakes up?"

"Not very, I shouldn't think." He squeezed my shoulder before leaving the room.

Resting my cheek on the back of Riah's hand, I tried to keep the tears at bay. Everyone was all right. Or, well, the friends I'd dragged into this were all right. At least I didn't have any of *them* on my conscience.

A short time later, Riah stirred.

"Hey, there," he whispered, as I popped up. "What are you crying for?"

For everything, I replied. For too many things to count. For... where was my uncle?

His head fell back on the pillow. "Man, I'm weak. Is this what it feels like to be normal?"

The door clicked open and his parents walked in.

I pushed back to give them space and went to check on Aster. She was awake now too, and her mom and brother were crowded in the room with Jeremy. We smiled at each other, weakly, and then I was pulled back out into the hall.

"Stella!" I cried, as she wrapped her arms around me. "Where've you been?"

"The Sentinel caught us. We had to give them a statement."

"You didn't leave when we did?" I tried to remember even looking for them when we were pulling off the property.

"No." She rolled her eyes to Ethan. "Someone was too interested in watching bodies be found."

He frowned. "They had dogs out, Grace. I wanted to watch the dogs work. Have you ever seen police dogs in action? It was so cool."

Stella narrowed her eyes at him and he backed up into Riah's doorway, which I'd left open. One more look from her and he slipped all the way in.

"Did you see them take Rich away?" I asked.

"Yeah, why?"

"He's not here."

"Maybe they took him to the hospital in Marinette. They can do that with dendrites, you know?"

Right. They could. Because our bodies were the same. Which begged the question, what could Rich have even found, if our brains were identical enough to not worry about being scanned and picked apart at a normal hospital? Nothing. Clearly nothing, if he'd been at it for thirty years.

I struggled with an overwhelming urge to vomit.

"Everyone's okay?" she asked. "What happened down there?"

"You don't want to know."

"Yes, I do."

"All right, everyone." Dr. Riley called, peeking his head into each of the rooms. "There are far too many people here. This isn't a hospital, we don't have visiting hours, and our patients need rest."

"Riah wants food," Ethan said, coming out into the hall. "Ask Aster and Chris if they're hungry and we can bring them back something."

Stella slipped in to Aster's room as her family slipped out, and after she checked with Christian, they left to search out dinner.

Dr. Riley raised an eyebrow at me from where he leaned against the wall, watching everyone file out. "And yet there are still three."

"I'm sorry, Dr. Riley, but I'm not going anywhere. Even if I have to sit in the waiting room all night long, you won't be rid of me until you're rid of Riah."

Six Sentinel came around the corner, and Dr. Riley cried, *"Out! Out, out, out!"*

When no one moved, he flailed his arms at them. "One person per patient," he said. "You can pick them up in the morning. They should have their strength back by then."

Chapter Seventeen

The Vampire Stereotype

The next night, I sat across the table from my parents, wishing I didn't know what I knew, even though I'd been hunting to dig up the past since the moment my uncle and cousin showed up on our doorstep.

My brother, who'd heard most of it from the cops and the Sentinel by this point, sat behind me on a stool at the counter.

It was just the four of us.

We'd been sitting in silence for twelve minutes.

My dad already knew his brother had been behind the missing girls. He knew I'd had some sort of run in with him. He knew he couldn't get a hold of him, or Nate, and that they'd both disappeared.

I'd spent all day at the clinic, making myself useful until my people were released, and now I had to tell my dad. There was no good reason to put it off any longer.

It would be easiest for me to share the memory, but as I sat there, across from him, I couldn't do it. If I did, it would fold itself into his consciousness and become his memory as much as it was mine. As if he'd lived it. As if he'd knocked his own brother out and possibly killed him.

So I used my words.

With each hit, he sank further into the gloom that clouded him every time I'd asked about his past.

Richard was controlling Nathan.

Nathan was controlling girls, bringing them in.

Richard was operating on dendrites to find the thing that make them special.

He'd tried to fix his wife.

He'd tried to fix his sister.

His sister. I used the word *his* instead of *your* to keep some distance from the horror for my father.

He'd killed those girls and dragged their bodies way out into the woods.

Who knew how many others in how many other towns, normal and abnormal alike.

My dad buried his face in his hands and I was weeping too. We all were. Justin was even sniffling a bit behind me. That's what it was to watch your father cry and ache in despair.

According to the surveillance from the truck stop, Nate had taken his dad's car and left town. He wasn't replying to me, either. He wasn't in contact with anyone.

This was where Justin piped up. That Richard Jameson had a possibly fatal injury and had been rushed to the nearest hospital. Only, he never made it.

Not that he didn't make it alive, but that the ambulance was back at the station the next morning and Richard was never admitted.

Justin was trying to figure out who had been driving his ambulance. Either he'd paid them off, talked them into letting him go, or they'd killed him themselves for what he'd done to the three girls.

Shady was small. Everyone was tied to each other somehow. Or their grandparents had been tied to each other.

Justin left out the part that I very well might have served the fatal blow myself. I appreciated that, but it wasn't something I could forget.

My dad spent a week in his bedroom, coming out only to attend the funerals.

He stood in the back, my mom and her parents surrounding him to buffer him from the dirty looks.

Those looks didn't extend to me, since Jeremy's story of how I beat off the big, bad dendrite grew and grew. Even if it hadn't, I was the hero and my dad the villain. I wondered if, had Rich died and we had a body to direct our anger at, or if Nate had stayed, my dad would have escaped that fate.

I sat dry-eyed at the funerals. Not that I wasn't sad. Really, I was too sad. Like so much sadness had hollowed me out.

There'd been a time when all I wanted was to be able to accept some amount of horror as normal daily life. I'd thought that in order to function in the abnormal world alongside fangs and full moon hunts, that a person had no choice but to gloss over some of the dark spots. But the dark spots kept piling up. There didn't seem to be an end to them, and finally being able to handle it didn't make me feel strong. It made me feel numb.

The one bright spot of it all, I supposed, was that sentiment of traditional Shady was on the rise once again. Lines were being drawn between those who understood the point of what my uncle had been trying to do, even while they disagreed with how he did it, and those who were outraged at the concept of trying to make anyone anything they were not.

I just wanted out. After everything, I felt like it was the only way I might be able to breathe.

~eee~

The day of the Valentine's dance, Riah got accepted into Madison.

This explained why Nora was in our formal picture—the three of us would be Badgers.

As the cameraman released us, she bounded off into the dimly lit gym.

It was darker than I'd ever seen it, the only light from masses of candles on the black-clothed tables and gothic lamps on either side of the band that filtered just enough onto the dance floor so you wouldn't trip over yourself. Almost everyone had gotten fangs for the occasion, and some had dribbled blood down from the corners of their mouths.

"How is it that even we have fallen to the vampire stereotype?" I asked, placing my own dainty fangs inside my mouth.

"That is so hot I cannot even begin to tell you." Riah looked at me, seemingly a little stunned, before popping his in.

I grinned. "Jeremy has a few tricks he could teach you with those."

"Boy do I." Jeremy winked.

Stella scooted over for my ritual dance tattoo—temporary thanks to siren tears—and I noticed the walls and tables were clear of their trademark silver for the first time. Maybe that's why it seemed so dark; there were no shimmering whorls and patterns to brighten the place up.

"Why is no one writing on anything?" I asked her as the liquid sadness from her eyes wriggled around on my skin, settling into the form she made of it.

"It would look kind of weird, don't you think? Happy sparkles all over the sinister vampire vibe?"

I snorted. "Who says vampires are sinister?"

Ethan and Jeremy both bared their fangs at me as Christian, Maribel, and Aster came back from the beverage table with a multitude of drinks.

"Polar bear, fruit punch, and something red floating in something else red," Aster said, as they set them on the table.

I peered into the silver goblet with the ball floating at the top.

"I can't wait to get out of here," Aster said, plopping down onto Jeremy's lap. "No more Sentinel trying to strong-arm the police out of a job..."

"No more council members asking whose side you're on..." Riah added.

"No more uncles and cousins and secrets," I muttered.

"Don't mind us," Jeremy said, motioning to Maribel, Stella, and Ethan.

We were split, just like Shady. Half of us leaving and half staying.

"It'll be nice to be normal again," I admitted. "Just for a little while." Or maybe a long while. I'd fought so hard to be a part of this community, to really feel like I belonged. And now that I'd succeeded, I was just...tired.

I could feel Stella's frown reaching for me. I'd promised her we'd come home so much that she'd get sick of us, and made her promise she'd visit so much that we'd get sick of her. I begged Ethan to take care of her, made him promise and made him swear.

But I'd been in and out of town before, and they didn't always make it easy. If the new council doubled down and the Sentinel had full police power, who knew if they'd even let us in.

Riah ran his finger in a circle around my knee. When he drew a line up the center, I imagined the fault lines that split my life:

normal versus abnormal, high school versus college, old Shady versus new Shady, Nate versus the world.

I had no idea where I'd end up, how Shady would land, or if Nate would resurface.

What I did know was that even if we weren't together next year, our roots were tangled, fused deep in the heart of Shady Woods, and no matter which way everything fell, the seven of us would always be tied tight.

A Brighter Day

I felt like I was behind a peephole, looking out into a place I had no business seeing, when I was only staring out the window at my new life .

Or really, my old life. A normal life.

I'd clearly been gone too long. At least Nora and Riah were with me. Nora was rearranging her things for the fifth time while Riah rifled through the pictures I'd printed to hang up around my desk.

Our parents had been gone for half an hour and we clearly didn't know what to do with ourselves.

I sat on Riah's lap and took the pictures from him to tape them up on the wall.

"I'm hungry," Nora muttered, turning the music down and spinning to face us from the middle of the small room.

"I'm always hungry," Riah agreed.

"I'm hungry when I'm nervous," she said.

Riah's fingers had been drumming along my thighs, and with this, he stopped. I smiled a little at my pictures.

"Grace, will you go get us something to eat ?"

Twisting on Riah's lap to look at her, I wrapped an arm around his neck. "Everyone's nervous, Nora. Everyone's new."

She bent a little at the waist like she was telling me a secret. "Everyone's not me." And motioning between her and Riah, she added, "Everyone's not us."

Nora was a siren and Riah a werewolf. I would mention to her that I was one of them as well, dendrite as it were, but I'd done this before—I'd been raised normal in Chicago and only spent four years with them in the hidden town of Shady Woods.

"Okay, let's go eat.

"I haven't met my roommate yet," Riah said.

"Yeah, he should definitely meet his roommate," Nora agreed. "Riah, go meet your roommate, then come back for us."

He'd been putting off meeting his roommate for the same reason Nora was putting off leaving this room. Riah's move in had been yesterday and his roommate's today, so he'd moved in, slept there, then made himself scarce ever since.

"You two will be fine. Odds are there are—"

"Twenty more abnormals on campus besides us," they finished.

With as many students that attended UW, odds were there could be up to seventy-five. We'd just accounted for how many abnormals lived wild and how many who grew up like us and would never consider leaving the safety of their hometown, though there was a high percentage from our graduating class who'd gone to college (an astounding total of seven). Which left those who hid in normal society, but not the ones in the shadows, feeing off of humans. The ones who'd grown up like me.

We'd been warned by those in charge not to find them. Why it mattered if we exposed Shady to more of our kind when they were still welcoming wilds to help keep sentiment between old Shady and this twisted new purist Shady even, I didn't understand. But there was a lot the town council—and the Sentinel—did that I didn't understand.

Old Shady believed, along with the governing boards of the vampires and werewolves, that we should stay hidden to contain mass hysteria and possible species elimination. Purist Shady believed we should live a little more out loud, which would mean letting the wolves and vampires hunt wherever they happened to be, no matter the carnage it might leave behind.

"Okay." I stood and moved to the door. "All three of us are going to meet Riah's roommate, and we're going to ask him to come eat with us."

"We can't do that," Nora said, eyes wide.

"We can and we're going to. Riah has to sleep with the guy, Nora. I think you'll be able to handle a meal."

She shook her head, eyes still wide, and Riah didn't move.

"You can do this. Trust me. Anyway, you have to do this. Trust yourselves." And I opened the door.

The one directly across the hall was open, and a girl jumped up from her futon and launched herself across her room, catching herself on the frame.

"Hi! I'm Mai. You should leave your door open when you're

home. My mom said before covid , everyone left their doors open."

Mai's corkscrew curls stopped moving a few moments after she did, and I smiled at her as she held her breath. See, I deposited directly into Riah and Nora's minds, she is just as nervous as you two.

"I walk around naked too often to leave our door open," Nora said from the middle of the room. Then, "What's covid?"

I winced on both counts. I knew what covid was because Charlie, my best friend from Chicago, told me all about it, every day for at least a year. But Shady had been spared—abnormals had been spared.

Riah let out a surprised chuckle, which turned into a choking cough, because he read the news in Shady and out incessantly. Most of the town residents, not as much.

Covid was a pandemic. Big deal that you couldn't not know, unless you lived under a rock. I don't know how to explain that without it being crazy you don't know, so... fake it?

"Oh! Covid. Sorry. Right. Covid."

I squinted at her. Also, do you walk around naked? Because this wasn't something we'd discussed.

"No, I don't, I just..."

She just didn't want to leave our door open. I nodded at her to cut her off. Don't reply to me out loud. Just think of me as a voice that... guides you. Mai wouldn't understand what Nora was responding to. She couldn't know I was a dendrite, any more than she could know Riah was a werewolf and Nora a siren.

Thankfully, humans easily explained away things they didn't believe were true, so she'd just think Nora was crazy.

For now, though, Mai studied Nora with a soft expression, and I tried to look at Nora like I was seeing her for the first time. Her stance was awkward maybe, to a fellow graceful siren, but to Mai, it was surely elegant. Swanlike. Nora's skin glowed—sirens were gorgeous, hands down—and her heavy black curtain of hair was as shiny and healthy as could be. Maybe that's why sirens were so much better looking than the rest of us—everything about them looked brilliant and healthy.

Another girl appeared next to Mai and crossed her arms. "You like to walk around naked?" This one was a brunette, with fake eyelashes, purple eyeshadow, eyeliner that followed the crease in her eyelid, a gold nose ring that matched the two looped in her hair, and—I noticed as she stepped forward to offer me a hand—freckles that had been drawn across her nose and cheeks in a perfectly spaced pattern. With, I was going to guess, the same dark purple she'd used on her eyes. "I'm Elody."

"Grace," I told her, accepting the handshake. "This is Nora and Riah, like Ryan but without the N."

"Wow." Mai strode across the hall. "You can see the whole campus from this side. All you can see from ours is the little courtyard." She kept moving for the window, eyes on the view, but as she passed Nora, she slowed and turned to her, as if caught up in a spell.

Really, it was just Nora's charm. I could feel it myself, but as often as Stella had used it near me over the past four years, it was fairly easy to pull myself from it if I wanted. As for Nora, it was only coming off her because she was nervous. To a siren, as one of our teachers used to say, proceeding cautiously was to slowly ooze charm. They didn't even really need to think about it.

Elody stalked in to pluck the pictures from under Riah's strumming fingertips. She shuffled through them. "Is blondie your boyfriend?"

"I'm her boyfriend," Riah said, snatching the pictures back. It read like jealousy, but I knew, again, that it was nerves.

"That's my cousin, Nate." His arm was slung over my shoulder, and I'd chosen the shot because of his trademark smile, cocky and irreverent all rolled up in amusement. It made me feel like he was playing a game, rather than completely missing, when I looked at it.

He'd disappeared last winter after I revealed some particularly nasty family secrets and smashed his dad's head into a banister.

Guess I couldn't blame him.

Also By J Mercer

More of the Shady Woods series

Shady Woods

The Little Wooden Box

Hands of Chaos

Other young adult novels

Triplicity

Perfection and Other Illusive Things

In One Life and Out Another

About the Author

J. Mercer grew up in Wisconsin where she walked home from school with her head in a book, filled notebooks with stories in junior high, then went to college for accounting and psychology only to open a dog daycare. She now writes women's fiction and young adult novels, freelance edits, and talks revision on The Novel Ending podcast. Her young adult novels have received multiple awards, and SHADY WOODS rated a perfect ten from the BookLife Prize, an indie arm of Publisher's Weekly. She wishes she were an expert linguist and enjoys exploring with her husband and two daughters.

For updates, news, and what she's reading, you can find her on Facebook and Instagram @jmercerbooks, as well as online at www.jmercerbooks.com.